ASHLEY BEEGAN

The Confession

To Sarah,

Because true friends are like big knickers.
They're full of support,
and cover your arse when you need them.
Love you.
X

Contents

Prologue

The package was much heavier than I thought it would be, considering the woman inside was still alive. Though she was unconscious, so I supposed she was dead weight. Sweat poured from my forehead as I dragged the load out from the boot of my car and allowed her to fall onto the muddy ground below with a considerable thud. A groan came from inside the bag, but I was confident she wouldn't fully wake up. Not after what I'd given her.

The crescent moon gave little light, and there were no street lamps this close to the lake. I'd driven away from the main car park and into Breadwood Nature Reserve itself. No one would see us here at 1:00 a.m. And having lived near the nature reserve all my life, I was confident there were no cameras and certainly no security guards. It was 540 acres of peace. It was fitting for her final resting place after a life of chaos.

I pulled out the wheelbarrow from the backseat of the navy-blue people carrier – a rental I'd picked up earlier this week under a false name. Which was much easier to do than I had anticipated. They barely looked at my cheap fake ID. The car had a large boot and a roomy rear seating area which folded down. Perfect for family camping trips. Perfect for dead bodies and wheelbarrows.

It took a few long minutes and a lot of grunting, but eventually I got the package into the wheelbarrow. I curled her body up inside it, though her thin legs still dangled from the handles. An urge to study her grabbed me, but a pang of panic threatened to take over. So, I grabbed the handlebars of the wheelbarrow and we began our final journey together through the ancient woodland.

At least it was a pretty place for her to rest, though the beauty was hard to enjoy as I forced the cumbersome wheelbarrow over the lumpy ground and frustratingly large tree roots. The handles slipped from my hand at least three times, and more than a few curses escaped my lips, but we made it to the lake in about fifteen minutes. This was quicker than I'd planned. The whole thing was going quicker than I'd expected. Though the worst part was still to come.

I teetered on the edge of the woods at first, staring out into the gloomy silence to make sure we really were alone. The dark curtain of water spread out in front of us, the crescent moon's light bouncing off the dark ripples of cavernous water. For a moment, I imagined being stuck under those ripples as the freezing water engulfed my lungs. The fear of being under there forever held me still. There would be no moonlight at the muddy bottom – just the ghosts and rubble of the old buildings underneath.

I dragged my attention back to the wheelbarrow. At least she'd have a ghost town to float around in.

I blinked hard, unsure at first if my eyes would even reopen. But open they must. I had to fight my way through this nightmare.

I turned back to the water and continued my search across the lake to make sure it was clear. It was empty of boats; as

I knew it would be. The district didn't allow night fishing in this part. And my confidence grew enough to step out of our hidden spot.

The hoot of a barn owl rang out across the water like a warning alarm. I rushed backwards, but the wheelbarrow slipped from my grip and overturned, knocking me farther into the forest. A tree root dug hard into my arm as I fell, and I cried out in pain.

Tears stung my eyes as I pushed myself backwards against the tree and listened intently. The silence was calming, and I took a deep breath to swallow down the throbbing pain in my arm. *Please don't have broken the bone.* I looked down at my forearm, which wasn't swollen yet. Though it certainly would not be pushing any wheelbarrows soon. Thank God I was left-handed.

I reassessed my plan. I could still drag an empty wheelbarrow back to the car. So, I just needed to do something with the body. Dragging it into the lake was no longer an option with only one working arm. She would have to die here.

I winced at the pain in my arm as I gingerly got back on my feet. Holding it against my chest, I searched the ground. A jagged rock caught my attention, and I reached out for it with my good hand. It was heavy. Perfect.

Murder weapon selected, I gently rested the rock down on a piece of leaf and turned my attention back to the wheelbarrow. It was already on its side from the fall, the woman within it still and silent. I rested my foot against her middle and pushed forward. She rolled once, and I pushed her again and dragged the wheelbarrow away. It was much easier than I'd thought. She groaned again, and for a second I thought I saw her move an arm or leg, so I stood back to peer at her. A fight was the last

3

thing I needed with my messed-up arm. I'd better be quick.

I grabbed the rock in my left hand and raised it high above my head. As if she knew what was coming, the woman suddenly jolted and let rip a piercing scream that rang through the forest. I almost laughed. *Who the hell does she think will hear her?* But I needed to be quick to sort my arm. So, I brought down the rock and smashed it against her skull. The sound of cracked-open bone splintered through the trees. And the scream stopped abruptly.

I put down the rock and ripped a hole in the black bag so I could inspect her face. It was tricky with one hand, but it ripped open eventually. Dark blood seeped out as I pulled at the opening to make it bigger. I wiped the blood away and stood back to admire my handiwork. The rock had crushed her right eye socket, and a flash of bone peeked out from under her skin. She wasn't so pretty anymore. Her breaths came in deep rasps, blood spluttering from her lips, and I raised the rock once more.

But the sound of nearby laughter stopped me in my tracks. I bent down to the ground and surveyed the path in front of me. The low mumbling of voices became clear, and they were getting louder with each passing second. I took a lingering look at the bleeding woman; she wasn't moving. I hadn't left any evidence. She should be dead within minutes. My job was complete. I heard a shout, closer again, and spotted shadowy movement a few hundred feet down the path. A group of young people were heading this way. I cut my losses, running off into the darkness with the rock in my hand. They wouldn't find her, anyway. The body would likely be discovered by joggers or dog walkers in the morning. But as long as she was dead, she couldn't talk, and all would be well with the world.

4

Summer

Summer Thomas shifted in the swivel chair, then crossed her ankles and straightened her chest. Holding her head high, she cleared her throat and took a deep breath. Detective Chief Inspector Jane Murray sat across from her in a dark suit and a white chiffon blouse. Swanson had warned Summer that Murray was cold and miserable, but she gave Summer a warm smile which wrinkled her cold, blue eyes. Hopefully that was a sign the job interview was going well. But it was difficult not to be intimidated by a woman as striking and confident as DCI Jane Murray.

"Summer, you seem really nice, and it's a big plus that you have your master's qualification in forensic psychology." Murray paused, and her smile fell.

Oh no. The nerves in the pit of Summer's stomach twinged.

She continued, "But I have to be honest with you about the role. This job isn't easy. You might have to analyse some quite-graphic scenes, or talk to people who have committed violent crimes. It might even involve crimes against children. Tell me, honestly, as a parent is this something you could handle?"

Summer smiled knowingly. These were words she'd heard before. People often assumed being polite and softly spoken meant she was incapable of confrontation or stress. It wasn't the first time someone had wrongly equated her being introverted to the same as being timid, and no doubt it wouldn't be the last.

"With all due respect, I handle it every day already. Some people I advocate for have committed the most heinous crimes this country has ever seen. Serial killers, paedophiles, rapists and stalkers who are all too depraved to be in the general population. I work with people who have murdered their family, even their own children, without remorse. Each day, I sit one on one with them in private rooms with no protection. I listen to their stories, their worries, their concerns and I help them. I make sure they know their legal rights. Even after I've personally been stalked, kidnapped, had my child threatened *and* I was slashed in the neck. Please believe me when I tell you without a shadow of a doubt, I can handle looking at pictures or talking to someone in cuffs."

Murray raised an eyebrow and smirked. "Good to know. I think those are all the questions I have for now, but we'll be in touch shortly."

Summer stood. "Great, it's been lovely chatting with you and finding out more about the role."

As Murray stood, Summer subtly wiped her sweaty palm on her black trousers and held out her hand. Murray took it in a firm grip, which Summer tried to match. She turned to walk away, barely able to contain the spring in her step that the interview was over and had actually gone well. Job interviews had to be up there on the list of top five worst ways to spend a Monday morning.

"Fuck it," whispered Murray.

Summer whipped back around to face her. Had Murray actually just cursed or was she hearing things?

"Excuse me?" Summer said.

"I'm going to recommend you for the role, Summer. I think you'll be a great fit as a resident forensic psychologist."

Summer beamed, her usually pale face flushed a light shade of pink. Surely it couldn't be that easy. She'd only just finished her master's and was now about to walk into the perfect job? Nothing was ever that easy.

"Really?" She tried not to sound too surprised, but failed miserably.

Murray laughed. It wasn't a natural sound; it was more like a short bark as if her mouth wasn't used to making the noise. "Yes, really."

"I don't know what to say. Thank you so much."

"Don't get too excited. It needs to be approved higher up. You might need a second interview with someone else. But I'll let you know as soon as I can, OK?" Murray's face was hard set again, and Summer could see what Swanson meant now about her coming across as 'cold.'

Summer nodded. "No, of course. That makes sense. Thanks again. I really appreciate it."

"You're welcome. Speak shortly." Murray nodded, and Summer took the hint to get out of the room.

She stepped into the whitewashed corridor beaming like an idiot, took a few steps towards the end and leaned against the wall. She was really going to work for the police. Well, most likely. Not definitely. Let's not get carried away. She took a breath and tried to push down her joy, at least until Murray confirmed it. She was so lost in her premature excitement that the familiar heavy footsteps coming up the corridor didn't even register to her until they were right by her side.

"Well?" Detective Inspector Alex Swanson's deep voice

shook her out of her reverie. His voice was in keeping with his bearded lumberjack look, and would have made her go weak in the knees the first time she heard it – had she not been looking for a violent missing patient whom nobody had ever heard of.

"She's going to recommend me to the powers that be." Summer's voice came out all high-pitched and strange. She cleared her throat.

Swanson grinned from underneath his ever-growing beard. "I said you'd smash it!"

"Swanson!" another woman yelled, her harsh voice echoing off the walls of the corridor.

Summer looked around Swanson's shoulder to see a petite woman with a dark bob and immaculate makeup standing at the end of the corridor: Detective Inspector Rebecca Hart. Unlike Swanson, her large voice did not match her tiny stature. Though it did match her attitude. Swanson had once accused her of having small-man syndrome and likened her to a chihuahua. The look she gave him could have made a man drop dead until he explained he'd meant loyal and protective.

"We gotta go." Hart jerked her head in the door's direction, her eyebrows pinched. She spotted Summer peeking out from behind Swanson's large form. Her serious face didn't change, but her voice relaxed a little. "Oh. Hi, Summer. How did it go?"

"Hi." Summer smiled back, used to Hart's short, somewhat unfriendly tone. "It went great." Summer was relieved to hear her voice had returned to normal, and she no longer sounded like an overexcited child.

"Where are we going?" yelled Swanson back to Hart, his own forehead creased and his smile gone.

"Come over here and I'll tell you. Not going to yell it down the corridor, am I?" Hart shook her head as though he was an idiot for asking.

Swanson tutted and turned back to Summer. "Catch up with you later?"

"Sure. My flat at nine tonight? Joshua should be asleep by then."

Although she'd had a few fantastic dates now with Swanson, he hadn't yet met seven-year-old Joshua. She was determined that they'd date for at least a year and be certain they'd want to be together before introducing them, but it was very hard not to want to introduce them now, just six months in.

Maybe that would be long enough.

How was she supposed to know for sure if she wanted to be with him until she knew what he was like with Joshua, anyway?

Swanson and Hart were now at the other end of the corridor together, and about to turn out of sight. She watched them disappear, muttering in low voices about whatever crime somebody had committed now. Maybe she'd be involved soon, if she got the job. And she and Swanson could discuss cases together over dinner. A wide grin spread across her face as she turned in the opposite direction and headed towards the car park at the rear of the police station with a serious spring in her step.

Things were finally looking up after everything unravelled last year. It had been ten months since a patient almost killed her, and she was unable to face returning to the hospitals for the first three. Now, she could hand her notice in and no longer have to worry. Maybe she and Joshua could move into a house with a garden. Maybe Swanson could join them.

The air was warm as she crossed the car park to her blue

BMW. It was only a one series, but she still felt a small sense of achievement every time she sat in the driver's seat. The radio jumped to life as she turned on the engine. She listened to it often in between visiting hospitals. It beat the loneliness of having no colleagues. A man was delivering the latest news stories in a droning welsh accent, and she turned it up as she heard the words 'violent attack.'

'—*woman has been found in Breadwood Nature Reserve. She was badly injured and taken to intensive care at Derby Hospital. It isn't known yet whether she will survive and no suspects have been revealed.*'

Swanson

Hart's heels clipped against the tiled floor of the station corridor as he followed her to the furthest door on the right, where Swanson had squirrelled away a small office for himself out of a disused storage room. Murray hadn't bothered to tell him to vacate it yet, but they both knew it was only a matter of time. So, they made the most of it until then. The peace meant he could focus. Or at least, he could focus when Hart wasn't around.

"Spit it out then, Hart." He groaned impatiently.

"I'll tell you inside," she replied sharply, eyebrows still pinched together. "It's nice to hear Summer got on OK. She'd be a big help."

"She got on better than OK. She thinks she's got the job." Swanson beamed unwittingly, breaking his usually stoic glower.

"Christ, I've only ever seen you smile like that around puppies. Is that going to be your new look if Summer is swanning around the place?" She gave a brief chuckle and opened the door to his makeshift office.

Swanson's face fell back into its more common scowl, though his cheeks felt a shade hotter. At least Hart couldn't see his blushing cheeks under his beard. He hoped.

11

"Don't be daft," he snapped as he followed her into the office and closed the door behind them. "Now, what's the issue you're being so secretive about?"

She sighed as she plonked herself down in a wooden chair which sat at the side of his desk. Swanson had purposefully made sure there were no other chairs in the side office when he first set it up. That way no one could interrupt him for too long. But the small chair had snuck in one day of its own accord. Which happened to be shortly after Hart had moaned about having to perch on his desk all the time.

"A group of teenagers found a woman at the nature reserve last night with her skull bashed in. Well, in the early hours of this morning, actually," Hart replied, her own face back to a sharper scowl.

"Is she dead?" Swanson asked as he took a seat in the battered office chair behind his desk. The same perfectly moulded chair he'd been pushing around with him from desk to desk for at least two years.

But he quickly jumped back up again.

"Have you been messing with my chair?"

"What?" Hart shook her head. "Of course not. I don't have a death wish. And no, she's alive. She's in hospital, but she's not in a good way."

"Someone's messed with my bloody chair," Swanson replied in a sulky tone as he fidgeted with the lever to put the chair back to its usual height. He sat back down, trying not to let his annoyance interfere with what Hart was attempting to tell him. "Probably the bloody cleaners. Where are the teenagers?"

Hart grimaced. "We don't know."

"How do we not know where they are?" Swanson asked, vaguely aware of how much like Murray he sounded, but

12

unable to hide his frustration.

"Well, the first two officers on scene were trying to help the woman, and the kids legged it as soon as they arrived. I'm guessing their parents didn't know they were there. We're talking about one in the morning."

Swanson sighed heavily, still trying to get the damn chair to the right height. "Mm. They were probably pretty spooked. Stupid kids."

"Especially if they were responsible for the crime." Hart gave him a pointed look, which made her bob fall in front of her face.

"You think they might have done it and then called the police?"

Hart considered for a moment before replying. "No. She was half tied up in bin bags. Fresh blood on the top part. Unconscious. I think they thought it was a dead body and freaked out."

"Poor kids." Swanson lowered his gaze. "That's gonna scar them for life."

"Yes, probably." Hart gave the statement half a second of thought before continuing. "So anyway, we need to find them and question them."

"Yep. We can do an appeal on social media. Whichever one kids hang out on these days."

"There's CCTV in the nature reserve car park. We might get some images of them too."

"Great." Swanson's hand ran through his beard. "Do we know how old they are?"

"The boy who called it in said he was sixteen, so I'm guessing they're all a similar age, most likely."

"OK. I guess we're going to the nature reserve then."

"I guess so," replied Hart, as she stood up and stretched. For the first time, he noticed she looked a little more tired than usual.

"You OK?" he asked.

She nodded and grinned widely before turning to walk through the office door. "Just tired after a late night."

"Do I want to know?" he asked as he followed her into the corridor.

Hart laughed. "Definitely not." Though she stopped laughing abruptly and her smile fell.

"What is it?" Swanson asked.

"I remember looking at my watch last night as I poured a drink. It was almost one in the morning. I was having the time of my life while that poor girl was getting her skull bashed in."

"Oh," Swanson said awkwardly. "Well, it's not like you knew, is it? Plus, whenever you're doing anything, someone is the world is dying. Someone's probably being murdered as we speak."

That didn't seem to be the right thing to say, because Hart didn't respond as they headed down the corridor to an exit at the back of the building. The door led straight to the car park at the back of the station, where only staff parked their cars. Swanson had parked his dark Audi in its usual spot in the far corner of the car park – protected away from all other vehicles. He brought up a hand to shield his eyes from the sun as he made his way across the bays towards his car. Hart pulled a pair of sunglasses from her endless Mary Poppins bag and gave him a smug smile.

She was back to her cheery self.

"I don't know why you refuse to wear sunglasses," she said.

"I don't refuse to wear them. It's just hard to find a pair that suits me which aren't black."

"Why does it matter if they're black?" Hart asked as she pulled open his passenger door.

"I don't want to look like a Man in Black wannabe in sunglasses and a dark suit, do I?" Swanson slipped into the driver's seat and closed the door with a soft clunk. Hart slammed her door closed so harshly that the car shook. He turned to stare at her.

"It's a car, Swanson. It will not break from closing the door," she said without looking at him, instead focusing on clicking her seatbelt into place.

It took fifteen minutes to reach the entrance of the drab industrial estate which led to the nature reserve. The car slid through a maze of oversized, grey buildings to reach one of three car parks leading to different sections of the reserve. This part led to the east side and wasn't used as often as the other two because it didn't show up on the nature reserve website or on Google maps. So only locals knew about this particular car park. Today, though, someone had taped the front section of it off from the public, and several marked police cars and white vans were parked near the far end closest to the reserve.

The car park was at least a couple of decades old, and the tiny spaces were roughly marked out with faded white lines. Swanson groaned. This was the worst type of car park to have to be in.

"There's a space." Hart pointed to the first available gap – between an old and battered Toyota Previa and a dodgy-looking black van that was probably classed as 'vintage' by some young idiot.

"Not likely," Swanson mumbled, and continued through to the other side of the car park, far away from anyone else.

15

He stopped at the very end of the row, where it was only possible for one car to park beside him. He took his time to line it up exactly on the barely visible white line so there was little risk of a car door being slammed into his own, whilst Hart tutted loudly and muttered something about wearing the wrong shoes for a nature reserve. Although she could hardly blame him for her footwear, she was still whining when they exited the car.

"I'm just saying, if *you* wore heels, you'd park closer, too," she continued as they stalked across the car park to the fresh police tape. Swanson removed his suit jacket and folded it over his forearm, the sun's beams too hot against his black suit. Winter was much more preferable to this muggy, summer heat. The UK buildings were not well equipped for such strong sun, spending the majority of the year protecting people from the cold wind and rain. A young man in a police uniform stood behind the tape, watching them with beady eyes as they approached.

"Christ, we've got actual children in the force now," Swanson muttered from the side of his mouth.

Hart laughed loudly, the noise reverberating off the trees which surrounded the quiet car park. Trust Hart to ruin the peace.

"You're showing your age now, Swanson," she whispered back.

"Morning," Swanson nodded to the child officer and flashed his ID, as did Hart. He nodded back, his floppy black hair falling over his eye as he did, and made a gap in the barrier for them to pass through.

"Come on, he was no older than twelve," he said in a low voice as they made their way into the woods along a man-made path. He hated carefully kept nature reserves with winding man-made paths. The natural hills of the nearby Peak District were much more fun. The air became instantly thicker as the sun bared down on the treetops surrounding them.

"He probably thinks you're about seventy," Hart replied, no longer attempting to keep her voice down now that the trees surrounded them.

Swanson pushed a large branch out of their way and motioned for Hart to go past him. "Me, seventy? Must think you're ninety then, seeing as you're five years older than me."

"Yeah, but I look better than you. Your beard makes you look older, you should shave—"

"Absolutely not. Look." Swanson interrupted her and pointed to the right.

Other officers had taped an area of woodland off from the far side, so the public didn't wander into the police search from an alternative path. They had taped most entrances to the reserve off, but it was impossible to keep everyone out as there were so many smaller entrances with no car park. One officer stood at the edge of the tape, watching over a trio of officers who stood grouped around a couple of trees a few metres away. Wavy black hair ran down her back, and she had a hard look on her face with one hand on her hip. Swanson recognised her immediately as Detective Inspector Lisa Trent, an officer he'd worked with a few times in the past. The gathering of officers was on the edge of the woods, and Swanson guessed that was where the perpetrator attacked the poor woman.

"Oh no," Hart muttered.

He glanced down at her; she was staring at Trent with a concerned look on her face. Though as far as he knew, they'd always gotten along well. Really well. He'd wondered a few times if there was something going on between them.

"What?" Swanson asked in a low voice.

She didn't reply. Swanson returned his gaze to Trent. She must have felt their eyes on her, because her head whipped around and she focused that hard glare on them. For a moment, she looked just as worried as Hart did, but then her face softened and she gave a wide grin and raised her hand.

"Nothing," Hart replied as Trent walked forward to meet them. "I'm sure it's nothing."

Swanson

Swanson tore his gaze away from Hart's frown and waved a hand in return to Trent. She quickly yanked her long hair back into a tight bun before walking forward to greet them properly. God knows how she did it so expertly in a matter of seconds. Where did the hair tie even come from? They always seem to come from nowhere. He'd seen Summer do the same.

Trent faced the ground as she walked, taking care not to trip over extensive tree roots on her way over to them. He couldn't tell if she was still smiling, but there was definitely the same strange nervousness about her that Hart showed. He hadn't worked with her too often, but she was an excellent officer. She'd always been so keen and took everything seriously. She was known to be overly intense at times, and not so much into joking around. But that was far better than not taking the job seriously. She looked up with a restless smile as she reached them, though her eyes darted around them rather than looking straight at them.

"Hi, guys. Did Murray send you out here, too?" she asked. Her smile sat firmly in place, but it looked like it was an effort to keep it there.

"Dixon sent us. Murray was busy," Hart replied. She didn't

bother to smile.

"She was in an interview," Swanson blurted out. He cleared his throat to hide the grin that threatened to take over every time he thought about Summer. She kept invading his thoughts, even when he was trying to focus on the case.

Trent nodded. "Oh, yes, she was. She told me to come check this out when she'd finished up."

"Oh, you got here quick, then," Swanson replied, mildly annoyed by the fact Trent beat him to the reserve somehow.

"Yes, I grew up close to here. I know the shortcuts." She winked at him.

"Have you learned anything yet?" Hart asked in a brisk, business-like tone. Swanson glanced at her, but she firmly fixed her unfriendly stare on Trent, who nodded in response.

"I spoke to the first attending officers. They actually left not long ago; you just missed them. But dispatch called them over the radio and reported an emergency call from a group of older kids. Teenagers. The kids were messing about and planning on sleeping out here somewhere." She rolled her eyes. "I assume without telling their parents. And they heard a noise. A sort of scream followed by a loud grunt."

"A grunt?" Hart asked, her face scrunched in confusion.

"That's what they said. Then they heard footsteps running away, and the girls freaked out. The two boys thought they were being funny by coming to the edge of the woods to look for the *monster*. Anyway, they found a body wrapped in black bags, blood everywhere and the face all smashed up."

"They're lucky they didn't meet the monster, then," Swanson said.

"Very lucky judging by the state of this woman's face. Well, from what I've heard, anyway. They called 999, reported the dead body and told them where it was, but at some point they hung up and legged it."

"A dead body?" Swanson interjected.

Trent shrugged. "That's what the kids thought at the time. Hopefully, they've seen the news and realise she wasn't dead, and come forward for a chat. The officers arrived, saw that the woman was still alive and got her an ambulance. Obviously, they had to rip the bags off to save her, so DNA will be tough. But forensics are over there looking for clues and the car park has CCTV, so we're waiting for that to be pulled."

"Any update on how she's doing?" Swanson asked.

"She's stable but unconscious. There was also a wheelbarrow found at the scene, so we might get fingerprints from that."

"A wheelbarrow?" Hart and Swanson asked simultaneously.

"Yeah, they think it was used to transport the woman through the woods."

"OK. So, we need to see the CCTV and track the kids down." Hart nodded curtly. "I'll get in touch with the social media team and see if they can help us regarding the kids."

"I'll check on that CCTV for you and keep you updated," Trent replied. "Speak later."

"Bye," Swanson responded. He watched as Trent looked awkwardly at Hart before turning away and walking off towards the path. Hart watched her leave.

"So, want to tell me what that was all about?" he asked.

"Nope. Come on, let's go check out the scene where they found her."

Swanson sighed. He knew better than to push it with Hart. He followed her through to the edge of the woods. Two huge oak trees sat at the edge like guardsmen, their middle branches touching each other like two swords. They'd taped a larger area off around them. Blood stained the ground in between, and the wheelbarrow lay on its side a few feet from the tree.

Swanson considered the scene, one hand on his beard. There was no blood trail anywhere other than the spot in between the trees.

"So, someone wheelbarrowed her through this woody section, right to the edge. At this point, they'd spilled no blood. Then they ripped open the bag and smashed her face in. Or just smashed her face in. I guess that action itself could have ripped the bag. It makes no sense, though. Why not kill her before putting her in the bin liners?"

"Why bring her here in the first place?" Hart asked.

Swanson studied the wild growth around him: the dry, summer ground and the rippling haze of freezing, deep water. "To throw her in the water or bury her. Surely there's no other reason to risk being here?"

Hart nodded slowly. "So, they were going to drown or bury her, and decided at some point to smash her face in. Maybe they thought she was already dead, but she moved?"

"Or they were just trying to scare her? Does she have other injuries that would suggest they hurt her prior to her head being caved in?"

"I don't know. We need more information. Come on, let's go." Hart shivered. "This place gives me the creeps."

Swanson looked at her in surprise. "It's just trees and a lake."

"Creepy trees stained with blood and an immense expanse of unforgiving water that would kill you in seconds," Hart mumbled.

He couldn't argue with that. The pair turned away, but Swanson's phone vibrating in his trouser pocket stopped him. He fumbled in the ridiculously small pocket to pull it out, but cursed once he saw the name flashing up.

"Murray?" Hart asked.

He nodded as he answered the call and continued to walk towards the car park.

"Murray, we're just at the scene now," he said, anticipating her reason for calling and hoping it would be a quick call.

"Great. But there's a man here demanding to speak to Summer Thomas, and I can't get hold of her. Is she with you?"

"No." Swanson stopped abruptly, and Hart tutted and looked at him impatiently. "Who is it? Why does he want to speak to Summer?"

"He won't give his name or tell anyone other than her what he wants to talk about. He just said he's done bad things and needs to tell her." Murray sounded mightily pissed off with whomever the hell this bloke was.

"Why has he asked for her at the station? She doesn't work for us. Not yet, anyway. Nobody even knows about the interview."

"He seems to be unwell. I believe he thinks she works as a spy." Every word from Murray was clipped and dripped with annoyance. If she was ever that mad at Swanson, he probably wouldn't turn up for work again.

"OK. Hang on. I'll call her." He hung up and stared at the ground. So many questions came to mind that he couldn't focus on one singular trail of thought.

Hart threw him a questioning look. "What did she want, then?"

"She said a man has turned up at the station saying he's done bad things. He's asking for Summer and will only speak to her."

Hart took a step back. "OK. And I thought the wheelbarrow

thing was strange."

"I know, right? Come on, let's go. I'll drop you off at the station to speak to social media and I'll check this guy out asking for Summer before I find her."

"Jealous, are we?" Hart asked with a smirk on her face.

Despite his worry, he grinned. "Yes. I can't help it. He sounds like such a catch."

They scrambled back through the woodland and to the main path. Swanson racked his brain for ideas of who this man could be, and Eddie Thomas was the only person who came to mind. Eddie was Summer's brother, and had been a resident of mental health institutions before. But he was doing better now and surely wouldn't think Summer was a spy. Also, he'd turn up at her flat, not at the police station.

"Hurry up," he called over his shoulder to Hart, who was now halfway across the car park behind him. He climbed into the Audi and slammed the door behind him, his thoughts now consumed with this strange unknown man and what he wanted to confess in private to Summer Thomas.

Swanson

D espite leaving his jacket in the car, the heaviness of
the warm air bore down on Swanson as he climbed
the short steps to the police station. His skin was
already becoming sticky, and it wasn't even lunchtime yet.
Thirty degree heatwaves were not for him, especially in a navy
suit. Freezing rain was far preferable to the humid heat they'd
endured lately.

He'd chosen to walk around from the car park at the rear and
use the front entrance, hoping to spot the stranger who wanted
Summer. It didn't take long. Immediately upon pushing open
the door, Swanson spotted him.

A scrawny man with thin, spiky brown hair sat in the corner
of the waiting area. He wore an oversized, navy raincoat which
had seen better days, and his eyes were wide open as he stared
straight ahead at a spot on the wall. He hunched over on the
purple sofa, with one knee bouncing up and down and his
hands clasped tightly together.

Swanson didn't take his eyes off the man as he closed the
door behind him. The man didn't blink, but his leg suddenly
stopped bouncing. Now he didn't move at all; he simply stared
at the blank spot on the wall. Though his lips moved ever
so slightly, no noise came out. He looked as though he was

whispering to himself.

Swanson tore his gaze away and walked over to the reception desk. The uniformed officer behind the desk, PC Charlie Marsh, raised one perfectly plucked eyebrow at him.

"Hey, Swanson. Murray said you'd be here soon. He's been sitting there for half an hour muttering to himself," she explained in a low voice as she tightened her blonde ponytail. "He won't move until he speaks to someone called Summer. We don't even have a Summer working here."

"Not yet, we don't," Swanson muttered back. "Did he tell you his name?"

She shook her head. "He just keeps asking for Summer whenever I try to talk to him. Even when I offered him a drink. He said she knows him, and he'll tell her everything. Who even is Summer?"

"Just someone who might work for us soon," Swanson replied absent-mindedly.

"How the hell would he know that?"

Swanson shrugged. "No idea. Are you OK to keep watching him while I speak to Murray? I'll be really quick."

She nodded and Swanson walked straight past the purple couch to reach the door which led to the secure section of the station. The area contained offices, interview rooms and the kitchen.

He tried not to stare directly, but he couldn't help glancing at the stranger as he passed. The man didn't look up, and continued to clasp his hands and mutter to himself. He clearly needed someone's help, but preferably not Summers.

Swanson used his tag to buzz open the door and stalked down to the large, open-plan office at the other end of the corridor. It was the worst room in the station by far, and caused mild annoyance every time he had to enter. It was created for teams to easily work together and share ideas, but it was simply too noisy and impossible to focus in there. It was yet another stupid idea from pen pushers higher up, some of whom had never even worked in the field.

Though she'd interviewed Summer in one of the special interview rooms off the main corridor, Murray's usual office was at the far end of the open area. He ignored the sideways glances from other officers as he stormed through and knocked twice on Murray's door.

"Come in," came Murray's voice. She sounded much calmer than earlier, though you never knew with Murray. She wasn't the type to give much away. It was impressive to watch her interview a suspect. It wasn't so great when you were trying to talk to her as a boss.

He pushed open the door and had to shield his eyes from the sun coming in through the window behind Murray's desk. She looked up at him, her nose wrinkled.

"What's wrong with your face?" she asked.

"It's just the sun." He pointed at the window.

She glanced at the window and shrugged. "Oh."

She made no attempt to close the blinds. Swanson swallowed down his annoyance, which was growing steadily since Murray's earlier phone call.

"Is the man still in reception?" she asked.

"Yes. He doesn't appear to be moving at all, other than muttering to himself."

She sat back in her chair and motioned for him to take a seat across from her. "And where is Summer?"

"I haven't called her yet," he replied as he slowly took a seat on the left, away from the awful sun.

"Why not?" Murray sucked in her cheek. He's at least learned some signs of her emotions over the years, and that was a sure sign he'd annoyed her.

He tried to choose his words carefully, but what came out was clipped and angry. "She doesn't work for us, so why would I?"

Murray stared at him. An awkward silence filled the air. "She wants to, though, doesn't she?"

"You want to put a civilian in danger?"

Oh god. Why wasn't his damn brain working? If he could have a minute to think, he knew he could talk Murray out of letting Summer near this guy. The whole point of her coming here was to be safer after her current job almost got her killed.

Murray sat up suddenly, leaning forward on her desk. Swanson instinctively leaned away. "Look, I like Summer. I want her to work for us, and I think she'd be great. But it was a struggle to get this position approved in the first place, and I worry if I don't fully convince them that Summer will be a fantastic help, they'll pull the position. This is an opportunity for her. It could really help secure her the role."

Swanson chewed over her words. If Summer didn't get this job, she'd go back to the same bloody job she'd nearly died in twice.

"Fine. I'll call her." He stood up to leave, wondering what Summer would say.

She would say yes, no doubt about that.

"Sit down," Murray barked, and he sat straight back down. "Call her now, please."

Swanson swallowed his frustration with greater difficulty this time, and pulled out his phone to call Summer. He knew Murray wanted to hear what Summer said. This was a test.

28

"Put it on loudspeaker, please."

"Why? You won't catch her out, she's as honest as they come."

"Prove it, then. Put her on loudspeaker."

Swanson hit the loudspeaker button and silently hoped Summer wouldn't answer. But on the second ring, she picked up.

"Hey, sorry I can't talk. I have a missed call from Murray, I have to call her back." Summer rushed out the words in a panic.

"No it's OK. I'm with Murray now. I know what she wanted."

"Oh? What was it?" Summer asked, the nerves clear in her voice.

Swanson wondered how to phrase their request. Murray's request. "There's someone at the station asking for you."

Summer laughed. "I haven't even got the job yet. Why would anyone be asking for me?"

"He won't tell us his name or how he knows you. He seems to think you know him, though, and you're some sort of spy for the police."

"Oh god, it's probably someone from one of the hospitals. What does he look like?"

"He's skinny, about forty years old, maybe. Short hair, kinda spiky. Dirty looking. Keeps muttering to himself and holding his hands together."

"That literally could be anyone. OK. I'm at home, but I'll be there within half an hour. Is that OK? Can you tell Murray for me, please?"

"Will do."

Swanson hit the end call button and stared at Murray as if to say 'told you she was trustworthy.' Murray grinned.

"Great. Don't look so worried, Swanson. Nothing will

happen to her here, will it? You can sit in with her if you like. Someone will have to. It will need to be recorded, and she'll need a briefing on protocol."

"I will," Swanson said with a determined grimace. Though the pit of his stomach was tight with the feeling that Summer should be nowhere near this strange man.

Summer

S ummer snapped up her grey handbag and ignored the funny feeling in the pit of her stomach, unsure if it was nerves or if the scrambled eggs she'd eaten for breakfast had gone bad. They were definitely a couple of days out of date, but she was pretty sure that wouldn't matter for eggs. Several patients ran through her mind as she scrambled around for her keys, but she'd worked with so many ill men it could have been anyone who was waiting for her in the police station. She stumbled over a pair of Joshua's trainers in the corridor and cursed; her keys were still nowhere to be found. She really needed a key hook. And a bigger shoe rack.

Certainly, none of the men she'd worked with knew she was at the police station this morning for a job interview. Only Swanson, her mother and younger brother knew that. As well as Murray and Hart. Unless an escaped patient was following her again. The thought made her stomach drop even further, but the glint of her key underneath the strewn trainers made her forget her concern. She grabbed the key and shook off her fears as she left the flat. Anyway, she'd know if someone had been following her. It had been pretty obvious last time.

Plus, she couldn't deny a part of her was worried that it might be Eddie in the police station, her older brother. But Swanson knew what he looked like, and he would have said if it was Eddie. He'd moved away to live with a new girlfriend down south, and it had been three months now since she'd seen him. But he'd video called last week, and he was happier than she'd ever known him. His mental health was much better.

As she ran down the marble stairs to the exit, she texted her mum to let her know she'd be late picking up Joshua. She knew Mum wouldn't mind. She was a far better grandmother than she had been a mother, and she loved spending time with Joshua. Murray had also texted her, asking her to park in the rear of the building when she arrived. The part reserved for staff.

A jolt of excitement ran through her as she left the building and jumped into her car, which looked in need of some TLC. Blasting up the air conditioning, she made a mental note to take it to a car wash soon. Preferably before Swanson saw it so she could avoid a lecture on the damage dirt caused to paintwork and how expensive BMW's were to fix.

It took ten minutes to reach the police station, and it felt strange to pull into the area reserved just for staff. She'd visited Swanson here twice and always parked in the larger, front area for visitors. She looked around as she drove past the bollards, waiting for someone to come running outside to tell her off as she wasn't supposed to be there. But no one came.

The nerves increased tenfold as she climbed up the front steps to the police station door, but it pleased her to see Swanson waiting outside at the top of the steps. He looked good in his white shirt and navy suit trousers. But he also wore a grim expression on his face and eyed her cautiously. Seeing him made her stomach flip-flop, which normally would be a pleasant feeling. It wasn't so nice on top of the nerves she felt.

"Hey," she said, looking up at him and shielding her eyes from the bright glare of the sun with her hand. She barely reached his shoulders, even in heeled boots.

"Hi," he replied in a low voice.

"Do you know his name yet?" she asked.

"No. He's in there." He pointed around the corner, towards the front area of the building where the main reception was situated.

"OK. Shall we walk in the front way, then?"

"Come round here first, see if you can get a look at him. Just in case it's someone you don't want to see."

He automatically reached out for her hand, but snatched it away as if realising they were at work now. She tried not to be offended as he led the way inside and she followed closely behind until they reached the end door. This led to the reception where the man was waiting.

The door was thickened glass, and Summer craned her neck to peek behind Swanson through the clear pane. The glass was tinted and it was too difficult to make out any specific detail. His outline was just about visible, as was a dark, baggy coat. It was impossible to recognise who he was from the steps.

As she stared through the glass, a part of her didn't want to go through the door. But if she wanted the job, she'd have to impress Murray, and this was the perfect chance.

"You don't have to speak to him, Summer. You can walk away." Swanson was always great at reading her. It was what drew her to him when they first met last year. Except then he'd thought Summer was the one with mental health issues, thinking she was being followed by an invisible person who didn't exist.

Summer turned back to look at Swanson. "No, I have to do

33

this. Anyway, I'm curious. I want to do it. Whatever he has to say, I'm sure I've heard worse!"

Swanson pushed open the door and entered the reception first; the man still didn't look up. Summer followed Swanson cautiously, though she made sure her body language didn't convey her nerves. She held her shoulders back, head straight and didn't take her eyes off the man. His face was pockmarked, and the aroma of grease emanating from him filled the sitting area. Summer's nose wrinkled, and she breathed through her mouth. Swanson stopped abruptly and turned to face her again.

"Do you know him?" he asked through the corner of his mouth.

Summer studied the man once more, but she shook her head. She didn't recognize him at all. Though there was *something* familiar about him. He definitely wasn't one of her patients. She never forgot them. Each one made an impression that was hard to shake off. Some good, some bad. Swanson nodded and turned back. She watched as he walked over to the reception and spoke to a pretty blonde officer behind the desk whom Summer hadn't met before. The blonde studied her curiously. She could just about hear what he was saying.

"This is Summer Thomas. Possibly our new resident forensic psychologist. I'm going to take her through to interview room one, can you do me a favour and bring him in for us in about five minutes? I just need to brief her."

The woman grinned and nodded. "Happy to be rid of him," she replied in a low voice.

Summer and Swanson walked through the reception - straight past the man. He still didn't look up at Summer. He didn't show any signs of recognition towards her at all.

Swanson led them into the back of the station once more, and they went into the first interview room on the left-hand side.

The interview room was small, but fresh and white. Very white. The lights were bright and there was a small desk in the middle with chairs on either side. The only seating choice was black, metal chairs with no armrests, and they looked seriously uncomfortable. Recording equipment lay on the edge of the table.

To Summer's surprise, Murray was sitting in one of the harsh-looking chairs, apparently waiting for them. Or making sure Summer actually turned up. She smiled at Summer, and Summer noticed Swanson raise an eyebrow in surprise.

"Summer," Murray said. "I didn't expect to have you back so soon, but thanks for coming in."

Summer grinned. "Nice to be back already."

Murray dropped her smile and cut to the chase – in what Summer assumed to be her usual manner if what Swanson said was true. "I probably don't have to tell you that this is highly unusual. Do you know who this guy is or what he wants?"

Summer shook her head. "I had a good look at him on the way in, and I don't recognise him at all."

Murray pursed her lips. "Are you still up for speaking to him?"

"Yes, absolutely," Summer replied without hesitation, despite the nervousness still pulling at her chest.

Murray nodded. "Good. I'll give you guys two minutes to chat before he gets sent in. Swanson will stay with you and lead the interview."

"OK," Summer replied, not sure what to call Murray. Ma'am? Sir?

"Swanson, come and see me after," Murray demanded.

35

"Yes, boss," Swanson replied.

Boss? Is that what she needed to call Murray? Not yet, surely. Once she'd gone, Swanson turned to Summer.

"So, I will introduce and lead the interview, OK? There are certain things we have to say during a process like this, and I don't have time to go through them all. But it needs to be recorded, and I'll say who's in attendance and try to get him to tell us his name."

Summer nodded, feeling completely out of her depth. Truth be told, she had no desire to lead the interview. She had a strange feeling of being stuck inside a dream she had no control over.

"So, all you really have to do is whatever you normally do when talking to patients to find out information. Easy, right?"

A choked laugh came from deep in her throat. Swanson whipped back around, giving her a strange look.

"What are you laughing at?"

"I don't know," she said in between nervous giggles. She swallowed down the laughter and cleared her throat, feeling her cheeks go pink. "I just didn't think we'd be working together so soon. It feels strange. And I laugh when I'm in strange situations – or nervous."

"You'll be fine." He relaxed his face, almost into a smile but not quite, and gestured for her to sit next to him. "Any questions?"

"No," Summer replied, and set her face straight again, cursing inwardly.

A moment later they heard footsteps and voices coming from the corridor. Summer immediately recognised the voice of the officer Swanson spoke to in the reception. She was saying something to the man about following her. He wasn't talking at all. It didn't take them long to reach interview room one with it being the first room in the corridor.

Summer took another breath and watched the open door. The officer came into view first, and she entered the room with her head turned away, still watching the man following her. He held his head down, shoulders hunched inwards, and stared at the floor. It was like he was trying to make himself as small as possible, as if he didn't want to be seen.

"And here is Summer Thomas, as requested," the officer said to him.

Finally, he raised his head. His dark eyes widened when he saw Summer sitting there. She actually felt the jolt of familiarity even stronger now with him so close. She searched his face again for anything that would reboot her memory, but whoever he was, his name was lost somewhere within her mind. The smell of grease filled the room once again as he entered.

"Please, have a seat, sir." Swanson gestured towards the empty chair opposite him.

The man did as he was told and sat down. He lay his grubby hands on the table, his fingernails full of thick dirt. Summer's stomach dropped as she finally realised why he seemed familiar. He was the spitting image of Andy, the patient whom staff at Adrenna Hospital accused of attempting to murder her last winter.

Swanson

Swanson shifted in the uncomfortable metal chair. He ensured his expression was neutral. One of the first interview techniques he learned was the benefit of positive confrontation. He wanted to ensure the man was comfortable enough to believe there was no moral judgement for whatever he was about to admit to – if anything had actually happened. He still hadn't said a word, even when Swanson asked if he minded the informal chat being recorded. So, he switched on the recording device and introduced himself, asking Summer to do the same.

"Now that we have Summer Thomas with us as requested, please can you introduce yourself for the tape, sir? Starting off with your name," Swanson asked.

"Yes. My name is Billy Bailey. I want to talk to Summer Thomas only."

His voice was higher than Swanson had expected. It was as if his voice had never fully broken as a teenager. It made him sound like a child, though he was clearly at least in his late thirties. Swanson risked a quick glance at Summer to gauge her reaction to this reveal. Her face didn't change or show any recognition at the mention of the name Billy Bailey.

"As I've just explained, I am Summer Thomas, Billy," she said, looking at the man with a small but friendly smile. "Just like the officer told you."

Billy Bailey finally looked up at Summer, but he quickly looked back down at the table. He closed his eyes tight. This day was getting weirder by the second. He didn't show any recognition of Summer, either.

Billy opened his eyes but continued to stare at the table. "You're definitely Summer Thomas?" he asked.

"Yes," Summer replied shortly. "How can I help, Billy?"

He hesitated before looking back up at her. This time he flicked his eyes up and down her body. Not in a sexual way, but as though he was trying to figure out if he could trust her with his secret.

"You know my brother. You worked with him in a hospital called Adrenna. He said you're nice to patients there and helped them. But he had to be careful about what he said to you because you're also a spy for the police and know all about the law and stuff. He said he hasn't seen you for a while and that you're probably here, in the station."

Swanson racked his memory back to the last time he was in Adrenna himself. Now that he mentioned the hospital, Billy Bailey did look strangely familiar.

"And who is your brother?" he asked Billy.

Billy kept his eyes on Summer as he answered. "My brother's name is Andy Bailey."

Swanson knew that name, but where the hell from? Had it been a patient *he'd* seen in Adrenna?

"Yes, I know Andy Bailey," Summer replied, "but I'm not a spy for the police as he believes."

"Then why are you here in the police station?" Billy asked accusingly, his eyes narrowed.

"Because you asked for me," she answered simply.

"Andy said they thought he tried to kill you, but you stood up for him," Billy said, ignoring her response. "He said you were the best one to ask for help if I ever needed it."

The recognition hit Swanson like a bolt of lightning. Andy was accused of slashing Summer in the neck and trying to kill her only nine months ago. He felt an irrational urge to tell this man to go away. Despite knowing Andy was innocent of hurting Summer, he was still deranged with a record for violence.

"And why do you want to speak to Summer today?" he asked. "What is it you need help with?"

But Billy once again directed his answer to Summer. "Andy trusts you. He knows you helped get rid of that doctor. He said I can come to you."

"Yes, Billy, so you said. But what is it you want to tell me?" Summer asked.

"I'm a murderer." He said it so casually, it was as if he was telling them he worked in a supermarket or a restaurant down the street. There was no emotion in his voice, or in his face.

Swanson risked another quick glance at Summer, seeing as Billy was paying no attention to him anyway, but once again there was no visible reaction on her face. She wasn't kidding when she'd told him she was good at keeping a straight face when it mattered. She didn't ask any other questions of Billy, though, and it took Swanson a second to realise that as the only police officer in the room, she was probably waiting for him to speak.

"OK." Swanson cleared his throat as he tried to get his mind back into the interview and off Summer. "And who have you murdered, Billy?" he asked.

The man let out a small noise, which sounded suspiciously like he was holding back a laugh. Swanson raised an eyebrow. If this guy turned out to be a time waster, he'd make sure he arrested him for that, at least.

"Is there something funny about my question?" Swanson asked.

"No. It's just that I've murdered more than one person. And I'm not sure who to tell you about first," Billy replied.

"Okay. Well, why don't we start with how many people you think you've murdered?" Summer asked. "And then you can tell me everything from the beginning."

The man looked away. His eyes lingered on the exit door just for a moment. Swanson wondered if he was thinking about walking out. His mind raced. This man had just admitted to being a murderer. But if he changed his mind or said he was joking, he could walk away scot-free. Swanson would have to let him leave if he gave no evidence or a confession.

"Billy," Swanson said in a sharp voice to bring the man's attention back to the interview. For the first time, Billy looked at Swanson properly without turning away. "How many people have you murdered?"

But Billy shook his head and looked back to the table. "I'm really not sure."

"Well, why don't we start with the first person you murdered?" Swanson tried.

"I'd have to think about it."

Talking to this man was like pulling teeth. Slowly. Whilst on fire.

Summer cleared her throat. "How about telling us the reason you decided to come and tell me about these murders?"

"I came here to tell you because Andy said you'd help me

41

stop. He said you're nice and you won't judge me. Because the truth is, I've murdered hundreds of people. And I can't *stop* killing them. Now, I've hurt someone I love and I've gone too far. You need to help me."

"How many?" Swanson asked once more through gritted teeth.

Billy stared at him, and Swanson felt a chill right through his spine. He'd interviewed hundreds of people, including murderers and sufferers of mental illness, but this guy's eyes were devoid of all emotion.

"At least four hundred," Billy admitted, so matter-of-factly and with such lifeless eyes, that Swanson felt like he was watching a movie play out in front of him. A bad movie with poor acting and a vomit-inducing horror storyline.

Summer

Summer swallowed to stop the bile from reaching her throat. She'd heard things before from patients, including stories of murder. Some had even committed filicide. But never four hundred murders, as Billy claimed to have committed. How would that even be possible? Especially for someone like this weak guy sitting in front of her. He only looked to be in his late thirties and was exactly the kind of guy she would cross the street to avoid. And she imagined most women felt the same. He wasn't charming like Ted Bundy or Paul John Knowles. Even if it wasn't women he'd murdered, most men wouldn't hang around him for too long, either.

Swanson spoke first, for which she was grateful. "OK, Billy. That's quite a big confession. Why have you decided to come here now? Why are you telling us this?"

"Like I told you. Andy said Summer will help me."

"So, you want me to help you stop hurting people?" Summer asked.

Billy nodded slowly. He reminded Summer of a guilty child who couldn't meet their parents' eyes when they'd broken the rules. Like when Joshua ate two puddings, or 'accidentally' stayed up reading past his bedtime.

"Have you hurt somebody recently, Billy?" asked Summer.

He hesitated, but then nodded again.

"Okay. Let's start there. Tell me what happened recently, please," Swanson instructed. Summer's mind thought back to any murder cases she knew of in the last year.

"There was a woman last night," Billy answered, his voice cracking as though he were upset.

Swanson tensed up beside Summer. She wondered if he knew of any murdered women already. Hart had seemed pretty serious when she called him over earlier that morning.

"I hurt her in the woods of the nature reserve. I bashed her head in with a rock." He looked up, and to Summer's surprise, his eyes were bloodshot. A single tear rolled down his cheek. "I loved her. She's the only woman I've ever loved. I didn't mean to hurt her."

Summer felt Swanson shift beside her once more. The words from the news reader earlier that morning came to mind, when he'd read out the article about a woman being hurt in the woods.

She decided to let Swanson question Billy for now. This was more police work than mental health, and far away from her usual line of questioning, which mostly revolved around the patients' legal rights, not their crimes.

"Who was this girl?" he asked.

"My girlfriend, Marcie. Her name is Marcie Livingstone. I don't know what happened. We were arguing, and she said she was going to leave me. Then everything went black. The next thing I know, I'm standing over her in the nature reserve. There was blood all over her face and a large rock in my hand, which was covered in wet blood. I heard some voices nearby, laughter, I think. And I ran away and left her there. Bleeding and dying."

"And she isn't the first person you harmed? Do these blackouts happen a lot?" Summer prodded, deciding she may as well butt in if Billy was going to force her to be there.

"Sometimes I blackout. Sometimes I remember every second." He shivered, as though something within his memory scared him.

"And who else have you hurt?" Swanson asked.

Billy sighed, as if about to start a momentous task. "I'll tell you everything. But first I need some time, and a phone call."

"OK." Swanson announced a break and stopped the recording. "Would you like a drink?"

It surprised Summer to notice Swanson stopped the recording so easily. Didn't police officers normally push through for information in these interviews? Repeating questions until they got answers?

"Just water, please," Billy responded.

"Sure." Swanson nodded and stood to leave the room. He jerked his head towards Summer to motion for her to follow him. She stood without a word and left the room closely behind Swanson.

"You OK?" Swanson whispered as soon as the interview room door was closed.

"Yes, absolutely. Just shocked. That's all. I mean, four hundred? Really?" She rubbed her stomach to pat away the nausea.

"Four hundred what?" asked the officer from the reception who'd poked her head around the kitchen door.

"Murders," Swanson replied in a grim voice. "Fancy doing me another favour? He needs booking in. He might be vulnerable, too. Possible mental health issues. But I have a few more questions and need to speak to Murray. Can you watch him for a few minutes?"

She sighed. "Good job we have you, then, Summer Thomas. Go on. I'll keep an eye on him."

"Thanks. His name is Billy Bailey," Swanson replied, and motioned for Summer to follow him down the corridor towards the open offices at the end. Summer had seen them once before during her visits with Swanson. He'd moaned about how much he hated them the entire time.

"So, what do you think of his mental health?" Swanson asked in a low voice as they walked.

"It's hard to tell. I think he probably did hurt his girlfriend, and he seems genuinely upset by that. There was no emotion shown until then. I don't get the feeling he's lying about that part. The rest of it, though? I'm not so sure. He doesn't seem capable of killing anyone and doesn't appear to have the intelligence to get away with it that many times. Unless he's completely playing us. Or lying."

"Why would someone lie about being a serial killer, though?"

Summer reeled off the plausible reasons on her fingers. "Attention, recognition, fame, mental illness. He could have delusions. There are loads of possibilities, really."

"OK. I'm going to speak to Murray. You can get him some water from down there, if you don't mind. And I'll meet you outside the interview room once again. Do not go in without me, though. Just stay with Marsh outside."

So, Marsh was the other officer's name. Summer walked off to the kitchen, which was a small room considering the size of the police station. There wasn't much space on the counter sides, as it was cluttered with kettles, microwaves and toasters. Empty coffee cups lay abandoned on every surface. A sign above the sink read, *Make sure you wash your own dishes,* with multiple red exclamation marks after it. Clearly no one followed the sign.

She opened one cupboard after another searching for some sort of plastic glass until she finally found a stack of paper cups in the far corner cupboard. Her fingers felt icy cold under the tap as she checked the temperature and poured glasses of water for all three of them. Swanson hated tea as much as she did. She threw her own empty cup into the bin and carried the full ones back to the interview room, trying not to spill them as she went and wishing she hadn't filled the cups so much.

Outside the interview room, Marsh was leaning against the wall. She smiled at Summer when she saw her. Summer took an instant liking to her.

"Hi, Summer Thomas," she said. She seemed to enjoy saying Summer's full name. "Seeing as our lovely Swanson didn't introduce me earlier, I'm Charlie. Charlie Marsh. But you can call me Charlie."

"Nice to meet you. You can just call me Summer, too."

Charlie laughed, then dropped her voice low. "So, four hundred murders? Is that really what he said?"

Summer nodded. "He might be having a mental breakdown, though."

"Let's hope so." She shrugged, right before her face dropped. "Not that I'd wish that on anyone, obviously! But that is better than four hundred people being murdered. Why has he come to tell you about them now?"

"Apparently he hurt his girlfriend last night and now he wants to stop."

Marsh's jaw dropped open. "He killed her?"

"I don't think so from what I've heard so far."

Heavy footsteps came from behind the women, and they

turned to see Swanson round the corner with Murray by his side.

"Summer, thanks for coming in to speak to him. I'm going to ask Hart to have a chat with the guy, along with Swanson. We'll see what we can get out of him before we allow you to speak to him again. Given the seriousness of his confession, we need to make sure we do every step properly and by the book. Good job so far, but for now you can go home."

Summer felt like Murray had punched her in the stomach, and for a second she froze, wanting to argue that it was her he asked for. But then she thought about Billy's poor girlfriend lying in hospital, and she knew deep down Murray was right. She'd heard stories of criminals getting off just because of one small error on the police's part. So she forced a smile and nodded. No way was she being responsible for messing up such an important interview. And from what Swanson and Hart had said, there was no point arguing with Murray at the best of times.

"OK. Ring me if you need me I suppose."

Murray gave a brief nod and walked off in the direction they'd come from, arms swinging by her side like an army major.

"I guess I'll see you later," Summer said to Swanson, who had a face like thunder. She handed him the two glasses of water.

"For what it's worth, I argued for you to stay with me," he said in a clipped voice. "He's only going to ask for you, anyway. So, keep your phone on, OK? No point going too far."

"It's fine. Murray's right. It has to be done properly. But yes, I'll keep my phone on."

She said goodbye to Swanson and Marsh and headed in the opposite direction to Murray, towards the car park. She needed to do something to keep her mind off Billy Bailey seeing as she had the day off from her normal job. Maybe she could go do the shopping? There was always something they needed from the supermarket and she needed to stock up on snacks before Joshua broke up from school for the six weeks of summer holidays. It was hardly as exciting as interviewing a possible serial killer though. The metal exit door flew open as she reached it, almost making her walk smack bang into another officer. Summer jumped back, startled.

"Oh, sorry," she said.

"Who are you?" the officer barked in a sharp voice.

Summer looked up. She was looking at a tall woman with dark hair pulled into a tight bun. Her face was not unfriendly, but certainly suspicious. Even if she hadn't been wearing the uniform, you'd know she worked for the police by her demeanour.

"Er, I'm Summer Thomas." Summer didn't know what else to say, so she left it at that and hoped for the best. The officer looked her up and down.

"Summer Thomas? Did a man come here looking for you?"

"Yes. He's in the interview room now with some police officers now, though. I don't actually work here. Well, not yet. Or at all – I just don't work here." Summer garbled, unable to get her sentences straight in front of the intimidating officer blocking her way out of the police station.

But the officer smiled widely and visibly relaxed her shoulders, her suspicious demeanour gone. "I'm Lisa Trent. Thank you for getting him to talk to us."

"Er, you're welcome. Nice to meet you."

"Nice to meet you, too."

Lisa Trent finally moved to one side and allowed her to pass through. Summer rushed across the car park to her car, whilst internally scolding herself for acting like an idiot on what was possibly day one of her new job. A desperation to be back at her flat crept in. Silence to process the morning's events would be better than shopping. But one thing was for sure, if Lisa Trent was to interview Billy Bailey, he would surely spill everything all at once.

Swanson

Hart's face was as sceptical as Swanson had imagined it would be when he explained what Billy Bailey had told them. She turned away towards the open door of his office, her face scrunched up.

"He said at least four hundred? Really?" she said after a brief silence. Not that Hart was ever silent for long.

"That's what he said." Swanson's own forehead was creased with confusion. Billy reminded him more of a child than a murderer. Other than his blank eyes.

"He sounds delusional if you ask me." Hart shrugged. "How could anyone get away with murdering that many people? Especially if he's as conspicuous as you said. What did our newest psychologist think?"

"She said it could be delusions, yet she doesn't feel like he's faking his emotions over Marcie Livingstone. I agree with that part. He seemed genuinely confused and upset about her."

Hart's head snapped back to the doorway. "What was that?" she asked.

"What?" Swanson followed her gaze to the door. There was nobody there.

"I thought I heard something."

She walked over to the doorway and looked up and down

each side of the corridor. Swanson followed, but she shook her head as she reached him.

"Nothing there. Never mind. I'm clearly going bonkers myself. Right. Okay. Let's go speak to him, then, and see what he says," she replied, walking away towards the interview room where Marsh still stood guard outside. The interview room door was still ajar – and eerily silent.

"I haven't heard a peep from him," she hissed as they approached.

"I didn't think you would, to be fair," Swanson replied. Billy was going to be tough to question to say he had chosen to confess to them.

Swanson walked into the interview room first, and Hart followed right behind him. Billy looked up, but he flashed an angry look in Hart's direction.

"Where is Summer?" he demanded.

"She had to leave. This is my colleague, Detective Inspector Rebecca Hart," Swanson said in a calm voice. He took a seat across from Billy.

"Well, I wanted to speak to Summer."

"As you were informed earlier at reception, Summer Thomas is not a police officer. You can speak to her some other time, as long as you tell us what we need to know," Hart replied in a sterner voice than Swanson as she took her own seat. "For now, we need to know a bit more about you."

Billy shook his head, and his dark, greasy hair flipped around his ears and the stench increased. Swanson remained grateful he hadn't yet eaten his lunch.

"I will only speak to Summer."

"Billy, you've admitted to murder. You need to speak to us. We are the lead detectives, and we can help you more so than

Summer can," Swanson explained, still keeping his tone gentle.

Billy shook his head again, even firmer this time. Swanson was once again reminded of a stubborn child.

"No."

Hart carried on with the bad-cop role. "Okay. If you don't want to talk to us right now, that's fine. We can't make you. We will come back later, but Summer won't be with us. It isn't her job to take information from you. Anyway, you might be lying and wasting our time for all we know."

"I am not lying," he said defiantly. He stared at Hart, his nostrils flared.

"Can you give us any evidence so we know for sure?" Swanson asked.

Billy didn't answer. He looked away from Hart and stared at the table once more. Swanson didn't prompt him again, but silently prayed he would speak up soon. However, Hart left it ten seconds before she piped up.

"That's OK, Billy. We'll see you again once they have booked you in and you've had a chance to get a solicitor. Let's go, Officer Swanson." Hart made to stand up. She was baiting him, and it worked. Billy's head shot up.

"No!" he shouted. He looked around the room, as if looking for a way to make them stay. Then his face lit up, and he smiled for the first time, showing yellowed, decaying teeth. "I'll make you a deal. There is one thing I will tell you. I'll give you some evidence to prove I'm telling the truth. But after that, I will only speak to Summer."

"What kind of evidence, Billy?" Swanson asked.

"A dead body." Billy grinned.

"That will work," Hart said, as if he'd offered an everyday item. "And we'll do what we can about getting Summer here again to talk to you."

Billy nodded. "Go to 136 Marion Road, in Long Eaton, and check the back garden."

"And whose body do you think we will find there?" Swanson asked.

"A young woman. I don't know her name. I didn't ask. But she's in the back garden and has been for about six months."

Swanson glanced at Hart, who gave him a barely visible nod of her head. They were heading to Long Eaton for his second supposed crime scene of the day. This was quickly turning into one hell of a Monday.

The Move - 21 Years Before

I looked down at my hand as it gripped the edge of the car seat, my knuckles had turned white. Not too surprising, given it was the longest car trip in the world ever. Even longer than the drive home after I'd been told both parents had died in the crash; and I didn't think any trip would ever be longer than that. The man driving was a police officer. His name was Ben something. Mum always said it was polite to remember full names but I don't think he ever told me his. He wasn't a normal officer, but some sort of helper officer to victims. Ben smiled a lot but kept coming to see me and talk to me about my parents and their crash, so I wished he'd go away. He seemed to think their car wasn't working properly or something; or that the crash wasn't an accident. I don't know. He was weird and always annoyingly happy.

Sitting next to Ben in the front passenger seat was Nadene Andersson; a social worker. I knew her full name because she wore a badge with her name and picture on it at all times. It hung from her neck on a long ribbon thing, similar to the one Mum wore when she went to work at the bank; but Mums was colourful and had M&M's with faces all over it. She brought it the one time we went to London from the official M&M store.

The best and brightest store I've ever been inside. Nadene's ribbon thing was boring and white, and constantly swung around as she spoke to me because she was always crossing and uncrossing her legs or moving about in her seat. So I remembered her full name as she forced me to stare at it so often. She was even more annoying than Ben. At least he was happy. Not that Nadene was sad, she just always gave me strange looks.

Neither of them had said a word for the past fifteen minutes, but they both kept looking at me through the rear-view mirror. I shifted in my seat and stared out the window, and squinted as the fields whizzed by. There was nothing else to look at, just field after field. Not even any other cars came by. Looking out the window normally made my stomach feel better, but not today.

It was strange being in a car now. I'd been in a car a million times before but it was different since the accident. It made my breathing funny recently, like I had to really concentrate on each breath, and my stomach flip-flopped all the way no matter how much I squinted out of the window. My hand ached from gripping the seat so tightly, but it was impossible to loosen my fingers. An urge to scream at Ben and tell him to pull over immediately brewed somewhere deep down. I tried to swallow it away, but it kept coming back. My breathing was so heavy by then they must have been able to hear me, because Nadene finally spoke.

"We're just around the corner," she said in her weirdly clipped voice. She reminded me of my headteacher; a strict old lady with short hair and thick glasses. Not that she was my headteacher anymore. I wouldn't be going back to that school. Nadene had similar glasses but longer hair. She was just as strict, though. She acted as though everything was my fault. As if I'd chosen to be here with Ben and her, rather than home with my parents.

I didn't answer her, but I looked out of the front window to see what she meant. Dad always insisted looking out the front window was good for car sickness anyway, though I'm not sure if travel sickness is why my stomach felt so funny. It wasn't the same type of car sickness I used to get.

Seconds later, the windy road turned, and Ben took a left down a dirty, tiny road. It didn't look like the type of road you were allowed to drive on, but he did anyway. Maybe the police could drive where they wanted. Not too far down the path, a wonky looking house appeared in the distance. But it was big, and my eyebrows lifted in surprise. It looked big enough that I could go to my room and live in it, and never talk to anyone else. That would be OK, I supposed. As Ben got closer to the house, he slowed down to miss some chickens that hopped around the road. I laughed, but instantly regretted it. I saw Nadene give me a stupid smile in the mirror and changed my face back to a scowl.

"You'll like it here, don't worry," she said in an annoying voice, still smiling. "There are two other foster children here, one boy and a girl. They're not far off your age. You'll like them."

Ben stopped the car, and they both got out. I waited a minute, suddenly not wanting to leave the car. I wasn't ready. Maybe I forgot something back at the station? Or back at home? My home. Not this stupid farm house thing, even if I did like the chickens. But my door opened, and Nadene's face was right beside me.

"Come on, you'll be OK. I promise," she said, and held out a hand.

I didn't take her hand, but held on to the door instead as I forced my feet to move. They were all heavy, and it was difficult to walk properly. Maybe it was a new type of car sickness. The fresh air felt good and made my stomach calmer. I loved being outside. You could do what you wanted outside. You could run around, or play games and sports. You could be loud or quiet. You could see animals pop out of nowhere or little insects pop up that you wouldn't see anywhere else.

"Hello," called a female voice I didn't recognise. My stomach instantly clenched again, and I held it tight with one hand as I turned around.

A lady with a chubby face, a big smile and a very round middle stood by the doorway of the wonky house. The smell of apple pies was coming from the doorway. I didn't like it. I liked my Mum's apple pies. That was it.

"Hello, Mrs Tilly," Nadene called back and walked over to the woman.

Mrs Tilly. What a stupid name. It even rhymed with silly. Mrs Silly Tilly. I tried hard to hold back a laugh, which resulted in me looking like I was actually smiling and Nadene beaming fiercely at me. Meh. Let them think I'm being friendly.

"Oh, aren't you a picture," Mrs Silly Tilly also beamed at me. She was much older than my parents. She had grey hair in a curly short style and wore a flowery granny dress.

"Say hello to Mrs Tilly," Nadene said with a giggle that made her sound unusually nervous.

"Hello," I replied.

"Come on in," Mrs Silly Tilly replied. She wrapped her arm into Nadene's and Ben and I trailed behind them as they walked into the house. He put a hand on my shoulder as we walked inside, and I struggled not to shrug it off. The front door led straight into the kitchen, and the smell of apple pie grew stronger. My stomach rumbled, and I silently willed it to shut up.

"Sit down, please," Mrs Silly Tilly gestured towards a table that looked about fifty years old, as did everything else in the kitchen. It was very brown, except for the flowery things everywhere. The table cover, the chairs, even the cupboards had flowers on them.

Ben removed his hand and took a seat. I followed and took a seat next to him. I didn't like Ben much, obviously. But suddenly I didn't want to be away from him.

"Now, she's eleven, right?" Mrs Silly Tilly said to Nadene as she busied herself with getting something out of the oven.

"Yes, eleven. She's very well behaved." Nadene replied. "She won't give you any trouble."

I kept quiet and watched as she put the pie on the counter and pulled open a drawer. "That's good to know, I'm sure we'll be fine."

"Where are the other children?" Ben asked.

"Oh, they're playing out on the field. They'll be in soon, I suspect." She sliced the pie and busied herself in another cupboard, pulling out plates and putting pieces of pie onto each one. "Here you go. Would anyone like tea?"

She walked over and placed a plate and fork each in front of Ben and I. I shook my head to tea, but picked up the fork. It would be rude not to eat the pie, after all. I took the tiniest bit off the edge with my fork just to nibble on. It was OK. Nothing like Mum's pie. Nadene walked over to the woman, and they talked in low voices.

"This is good, eh?" Ben said, nudging me with his elbow.

"Mmm," I replied, pretending my mouth was full and wishing he'd be quiet so I could hear what they were saying. All I could hear was the odd word, like 'accident', and 'quiet', and something about a path.

"Oh, here they are!" Mrs Silly Tilly raised her voice as she went to open the kitchen door. Two children walked in, a boy and a girl just like Nadene said. The boy was much smaller than the girl. His welly boots were thick with mud and he looked about nine years old. He smiled at me but looked nervous. I was eleven, and he was definitely younger than me. The girl was very pretty, but skinny. Her welly boots were muddy too, and her cheeks pink. Blond hair fell down her back. She didn't smile.

"Come on in, say hello. This is Billy," Nadene waved him in first and put her hands around his shoulders. "And this-"

The girl cut her off. "My name is Lauren," she replied.

"Oh, Lauren?"

"She keeps changing her name," Mrs Silly Tilly replied with a laugh. "It's hard to keep up!"

Lauren looked me up and down. She didn't smile, but I liked her. I could tell we were going to be friends already.

"Now, go and get your boots off kids." Mrs Silly Tilly called over to them. Ben got up and walked over to them so now the three of them were talking in low voices. Billy and Lauren walked over to a door at the end of the kitchen, I watched them as they walked. They kept their heads down, Lauren held Billy's hand. I wondered if they were brother and sister. As they reached the door, hidden from the adults, they both turned to look at me. Lauren mouthed something, but I couldn't make it out.

"What?" I mouthed back with a furrowed brow.

She exaggerated her lips further, and this time I had no trouble making it out.

"Run."

Swanson

The town of Long Eaton sat on the north banks of the River Trent, on the border between Nottinghamshire and Derbyshire. A market town famous for lace-making, not murderers. It was only twenty minutes from Derby up the A52, but thanks to road works it took Swanson thirty minutes to reach Marion Road. The plan decided with Murray was for Swanson and Hart to check it out together and call for forensics if anything was found. Billy was waiting at the station. He wasn't quite under arrest yet, as they needed to establish if he was a murderer or needed psychiatric help. But he would certainly find it difficult if he tried to leave the station before their update.

It was late afternoon now, and the sun sat heavily in the sky in a way that meant it was shining in Swanson's eyes no matter where he looked as he tried to drive. Hart was right, he really did need some sunglasses even if only for the car.

Marion Road was a long, winding road on the edge of the Shamly estate. Red brick 1960s houses filled the road with long plots of land and multiple-car driveways. A sign of the good old days when the councils built proper houses with good sized plots of land. Not like the new builds these days, which would fall down if you blew on them too hard.

"You know these houses all have those really long back gardens, don't you?" Hart asked miserably. "It's going to be tricky to get permission just to dig it up on a whim."

Number 136 was at the end of the road on a large corner plot, however, which gave Swanson hope that the back garden might not be as large as the others on the street. He pulled up outside, parking on the pavement and ignoring the driveway, which was easily big enough for six cars. Parking on someone's driveway was an easy way to annoy them before even saying hello. The sound of children's shouts and laughter greeted them as they got out of his car, thanks to a field opposite with a kids park and concreted sports arena. He made sure he pulled the car up on the pavement as much as it could be whilst still allowing a wheelchair to pass, and he double checked the wing mirrors were fully folded in.

"There must be fifty kids over there!" Hart remarked with a wrinkled nose. "I could never live so close to a park with all that noise."

"You're such a grouch. You'll end up as an old, single cat lady, you know."

Hart had already rescued three cats in as many years from a nearby shelter. Which, as a dog person, Swanson struggled to understand. Cats had zero appeal to him. Though Hart's attitude was similar to a cat, now he thought about it.

"As amazing as that would be, I am actually not single. I'm seeing somebody, remember?" she replied with a snooty, catlike undertone.

"So you say," Swanson teased. Hart had refused to give him any information when he'd asked whom she'd been texting. The look on her face said it all, though. She was loved up hard with someone.

They continued their walk up the oval-shaped driveway, and Swanson rapped his knuckles on the white front door. The small porch was covered in bugs and cobwebs. Whoever lived here certainly wasn't overly house-proud.

It didn't take long to hear shuffling on the other side, and within thirty seconds the door creaked open to reveal an elderly gentleman. He was easily in his eighties, mostly bald with a neck which looked too skinny to hold up such a colossal head. He stared at them with the usual suspicious look they were greeted with when knocking somewhere unannounced. It was the suits. Though it got a better reception than uniforms.

"Hello, sir. I'm Detective Inspector Alex Swanson, and this is my colleague Detective Inspector Rebecca Hart."

He flashed his ID, as did Hart, and watched the man's response. This was where he might slam the door in their faces, or worry they were there to give him bad news.

"Oh! I see. How can I help?" he asked, looking more worried than annoyed. A good sign that he wasn't scared of the police and would hopefully talk openly to them.

"We'd just like to talk to you. Can we please come in, sir?" Hart asked.

"Is there something you need to tell me? Has something happened?" The man's blue eyes widened in fear.

"No," Swanson replied firmly. "As far as we know nothing has happened to anybody you know. We want to talk to you about your house."

"OK. Well, yes, of course. You're welcome inside." He smiled now, clearly relieved by Swanson's reassurance.

Swanson stepped inside onto a soft, Jacobean red carpet – the typical style of everyone in the UK over eighty, it seemed. He was careful not to get too close to the fireguard, which was covered in what appeared to be small, easily breakable antique ornaments. He silently hoped Hart had also spotted them, as she was much more prone to clumsiness than he was.

"You two make yourselves comfortable in here," the man said, gesturing to his left into the living room, which had the same headache-inducing carpet and a scuffed brown sofa. "And I'll get tea and biscuits."

Swanson almost told him there was no need, but thought better of it. Tea might help the old man take their news better. The thought of trying to stomach a cup of tea himself right now, though, was enough to make him nauseous.

"OK," Swanson replied. "Please, can mine just be water?"

"If that's what you'd like," the man replied with a smile. Swanson was warming to him already.

He and Hart tried to perch on the brown sofa in a professional pose, but it was so soft they sank straight into it. Swanson stood instead and surveyed the room. More valuable knickknacks covered the fireplace and shelves, along with photos of many people. He searched for Billy in the photos whilst the man clanged about in the kitchen, but he didn't appear to be in any of them. The man returned within a few minutes with a tray which had two cups of tea and a glass of water, along with milk, sugar and biscuits.

"There you go, dear," he said to Hart as he plonked the tray onto the coffee table in front of her. "I thought you could add milk and sugar to your own preference. My wife would normally make it for guests, you see. But she passed on six months ago."

"Sorry for your loss, sir," Hart replied.

"Yes, it is lonely without her, I must admit. But anyway, you two had something you wanted to talk to me about?"

65

"Yes, sir. Could I ask your name?" Swanson began. Hart was busy adding far too much sugar to her cup of tea.

"Of course. It's Gord. Gordon Blacksmith," Gordon tipped his head as though introducing himself in a formal party.

"And how long have you lived at this address, Mr Blacksmith?" Swanson continued as Hart added the tiniest splash of milk.

"Please, call me Gord. Well, Edith and I moved in here after our son got married." Gordon scratched his chin. "That would make it about six years."

Swanson and Heart glanced at each other. The man had said he'd murdered somebody six months ago at this address, yet Gordon would have been living here.

"Does anybody else live here?" Hart finally joined in the conversation now her tea was complete.

The man shook his head. "No, just me since Edith died."

"It's quite a big house for just one person," Hart remarked.

"My son lived with me, dear. But he's moved out."

"Oh, I see. What's your son's name, out of interest?" Swanson asked.

"Gary Blacksmith. Why?"

Swanson and Hart shared a glance. They were going to have to come out with it, eventually.

"Gordon, somebody has told us they buried a body in your back garden. It would have been six months ago," Hart spat out.

Gordon's eyes grew wide, but then he snorted with laughter. "Oh, I think they're winding you up, love."

"Yes, they might be. But we need to know for sure," Swanson explained.

Gordon's smile fell. "Who was it who said this?" he asked.

"He said his name is Billy Bailey," Swanson replied.

Gordon looked away. He appeared to be deep in thought. "Billy Bailey? I've never heard of him. Does he know me?"

"He didn't say. Unfortunately, he wouldn't give us any more details. Could we see your garden, maybe? Just to have a look," Swanson asked.

"Sure. I don't see why not," replied Gordon, standing shakily.

He led them through the tiny kitchen and out of the back door of the property. They stepped into a fairly big back garden, though it wasn't as long as Swanson had worried. It had a tall fence, so it was quite private from other gardens and houses on the block. Swanson strolled down the concrete path in the middle of two grassy verges.

"So, you did live here six months ago, Gordon? Just to confirm," Swanson asked as he surveyed the garden.

"Like I said, my Edith died about six months ago. So yes, I lived here. Though I stayed with my son for a bit straight after her death. Just a couple of weeks to get my head around what had happened. It was cancer, but it took her quickly. It took me some time to return here without her, if I'm honest." Gordon hung his head, a sad smile lining his face.

Swanson nodded. He reached a patch of grass that stood out and cocked his head to one side to focus on it. The blades of grass were a shade darker than the rest of the garden.

"Can I ask what happened here, Gordon?" he called over.

"Oh, that's from a few months ago. There was a big messy patch right there. It was huge! I assume a fox or something tore up the garden. It took me ages to get it all straightened out, but as you can see, it isn't perfect. I found it when I came back from staying away after Edith's passing, actually. It gave me something to focus on, at least."

As soon as the words were out of his mouth, Gordon's face paled. His eyes opened wide in horror, and Swanson reached for his phone to call Murray as Hart asked Gordon to follow her back inside and talk her through exactly what had happened after Edith's death.

Summer

Summer swiped open her phone to make sure she hadn't missed a call or text message from Swanson. But there'd been nothing since she last checked it; five minutes ago. She sighed and sank further into the sofa as she gazed around her living room. Joshua had thrown cushions on the floor and strewn his blanket across them. A giant toy truck was abandoned in front of the TV, along with other toys dotted around the place. Summer contemplated tidying up, but she couldn't decide where to start. So, her thoughts soon fell back to Billy Bailey and his brother, Andy.

Though they had accused Andy of stabbing her in the neck, he wasn't actually the guilty party. He was ill, though, hence why he was in a psychiatric hospital. She hadn't visited Adrenna since the incident. It was *'closed for refurbishment'* following a grizzly discovery by Swanson and Hart.

As far as Summer could remember, Andy suffered from catatonic schizophrenia. A severe mental disorder which caused bouts of significant reduction of movement or mutism. Someone suffering from catatonia might stare at a wall for hours at a time without moving a muscle, and without talking or responding to other people's actions. She'd seen Andy in a catatonic state on the ward at Adrenna Hospital before, but had never seen him violent. As far as she knew, he'd never been violent to anyone other than himself. Like most of her patients. She couldn't even check now the hospital was closed. Not that she would want to set foot on that ward again after what happened there.

An idea came to her which made her sit up straight on the sofa. Maybe one of the nurses from Andy's ward would know about Billy Bailey. If he had been speaking to Andy, then the staff would know. They supervised both visits and phone calls in Adrenna, and Summer was very close to one particular nurse – Aaron Walker. Her old university friend, who almost became more than a friend last year. He worked as a nurse at Adrenna at the same time as she did and was partly responsible for saving her life that day. He would know if anyone had been visiting Andy.

She sat forward on the sofa, closed her eyes and thought hard to imagine Andy's face. He and Billy had the same scrawny faces and thin, dark hair. He talked little, and staff often found him in a catatonic state in the living area of the ward. Therefore, he hadn't spoken too much to her. God only knew why he had told his brother about her. The whole thing was strange. Unless Andy had sent Billy to find out what she looked like now, or maybe even to hurt her to get revenge after they accused him of slashing her?

She groaned and rested her face in her hands. This was where being followed around by patients and stabbed got you. A paranoid mess. If only Swanson would call so they could talk it through. She checked her phone again – nothing.

If Swanson wouldn't call, Aaron would have to do. She brought up Aaron's number and hit dial. His phone rang and rang. Her knee bounced up and down nervously as she waited for him to answer. She held her leg still with her free hand and silently cursed her long-deceased father for the annoying habit. She lowered the phone away from her ear, but a small voice piped up just before she hung up.

"Summer?"

The phone flew back to her ear. "Aaron? Hey, yes, it's me,"

"Well, this is a surprise! How are you?" He sounded out of breath, as though he'd run somewhere to take the call.

"I'm OK, thanks. I thought we could have a catch-up?" Guilt settled in as she realised she hadn't called him in weeks, and was now only calling for a favour.

"Sure, that would be great. When were you thinking?"

The guilt increased hearing how excited he sounded to see her. She stood and paced the living room.

"Er, now?" she asked nervously.

"Right now?"

"Yes. Confession time, I have something to chat with you about. It's kinda urgent." Summer held her breath.

"Well, that sounds ominous, Summer! But, OK. I'm doing some community nursing whilst Adrenna is closed, but I have a lunch break in an hour. We'll have to meet at that farm cafe near me so I can get back to my shift on time. Does that suit you?"

"Perfect! Thank you, Aaron. I knew I could rely on you. See you soon!" She hung up and perched again on the sofa, head in her hands, and prayed Aaron would have a clue which made this whole ridiculous situation fit together.

Swanson

S wanson stood guard next to the fresh patch of grass, with one hand on his forehead to rub away the ache that had gathered there. Though it did little for the pain. He squeezed his eyes shut tight and reopened them as if that would help dull the ache. It didn't. He sighed and tried to focus. His body was probably in need of a simple drink. Nothing more, nothing less. But after last year's diagnosis of a brain tumour, headaches caused a certain level of new anxiety.

He turned to look at the shed a few feet away, where Gordon Blacksmith's sizable backside greeted him. Hart stood outside the shed. Gordon had kindly offered them a spade to dig a small portion of the fresh grass up. He'd said this was to confirm there was no dead body buried in his garden. Though he had paled for a split second after confirming he found a hole in his garden six months ago, it took approximately ten seconds for him to go into adamant denial.

"There's lots of foxes round here, see," he informed them as he clanged around in his shed. "You don't see them in the day, mind. I'm not sure where they hide during the day. But you do see them running around that field at night time looking for food."

Hart threw Swanson a glance, one eyebrow raised. No

one would ever know she was nervous by looking at her, but after so long working together, Swanson knew she'd be feeling sick with apprehension right about now. Finding dead bodies would do that to most people, but Hart was particularly terrified of it since they'd found an enormous pile of bodies last year. The smell still felt like it was stuck in his nostrils sometimes. Especially at night.

"Ah, here it is," Gordon called out. He emerged seconds later, backside first, and turned to reveal a small shovel. "I suppose you want to do it?"

He directed this question to Swanson, but Hart stepped forward before he had a chance to answer.

"I'll do it, Gordon." She grabbed the shovel from him, who gave her a surprised look but said nothing.

Clever man. Hart might hate finding dead bodies, but she wouldn't allow anyone to be sexist in front of her – old or not. She dug the shovel into the dry soil – just a couple of inches to get the top layer of grass off. She was careful as she could be, with Gordon watching every move. He chewed his lip as he watched her dig. She repeated the process a few times to create a dip about a foot wide to start with, then dug down deeper into the soil.

"That's about how deep it was when the fox came," Gordon called out when she'd dug down a foot or so.

Hart put down the shovel, pulled on some gloves from her bag and pulled out clumps of dirt with her hands instead. She put a flat hand in the soil and looked up at Swanson, her eyes wide. He knew that look. He bent down and tugged on his own gloves as she pulled back a last handful of soil. A small piece of material stuck out of the ground. Dirt clung to it, but as Swanson fingered it softly, it had a nylon feel and a red sheen to it. He guessed it to be a piece of a red anorak.

"It could be anything yet, but let's call in the specialists so we don't mess anything up," Swanson said, loud enough for Gordon to also hear. Murray had asked for evidence before calling in any specialists, so hopefully this would be enough.

"OK," Hart agreed, but she continued to brush soil off the red material. It became apparent the material was certainly some sort of cuff to a jacket. Swanson reached a hand out to stop her.

"Leave it to the team, Hart," he said, hoping she would realise he didn't want the old man to see a body. His last six months had been hard enough, and knowing he'd unwittingly helped to bury a body in his backyard wouldn't exactly help. Hart stared at him with annoyance, but he moved his eyes toward Gordon. Her expression softened, and she nodded and took out her phone to call Murray.

"Let's have a cup of tea, Gordon. Why don't you give your son a call?" Swanson stood and led the old man back inside, dreading the thought of having to stomach a whole cup of tea.

Summer

It took a little over half an hour to drive to the farm cafe, which lay a mile past Adrenna Hospital. Aaron had moved nearby once he landed a job there, though Summer wasn't exactly sure where he lived.

The winding, country roads to the farm made Summer's heart pound in her chest. Her sweaty hands gripped the steering wheel despite blasting the air conditioning. She hadn't driven down these roads since she almost died last year. By the time she pulled into the small car park of the cafe, her knuckles were white. She carefully ungripped the steering wheel and stretched out her aching fingers. She stared at the building in front of her, reminding her brain that she was not going to Adrenna. She was going to see Aaron, and then go home.

Once she could breathe normally again, she left her BMW and walked along the dirt trail to the entrance. It was at the front of an old working farm, but the building itself was quite modern. It was a bit out of place with the older farm buildings, but nice enough.

The front wall was almost all glass, and she spotted Aaron's skinny form and floppy black hair sitting close to the oversized window. She'd met Aaron here before, though that meeting hadn't gone so well. Hopefully that bad karma wasn't indicative of how this meeting would go.

Inside the cafe, the smell of baked pastries and sweet cakes made Summer's stomach rumble as she realised she'd forgotten to eat breakfast in all the drama of the morning. As she approached, Aaron smiled and pointed at a fresh cheese toastie lying on the table across from him. The melted cheese spilled over the edge of the thick bread and instantly made her mouth water.

"Aw, you didn't need to do that!" she said as she took a seat across from him, trying not to scrape it along the floor. "I'm super grateful, though. I'm starving. This day has been about fifty-six hours long already. Thank you."

"You're welcome!" He grinned again, showing off perfect, white teeth. Aaron spoke theatrically and had an air of Captain Jack Sparrow about him. He definitely should've been an actor. "I'm really glad you called."

"Me too." Summer smiled. "It's great to see you."

Aaron tucked into his own toastie, and Summer followed suit. She could barely get the sandwich in her mouth fast enough. The melted cheese and crisp toast tasted amazing.

"Careful you don't eat your hand!" Aaron raised an eyebrow at her.

Summer swallowed the large mouthful of food. "Sorry! I didn't realise how hungry I was until I walked in here. So, how have you been?" she asked.

He cocked his head to one side, as if unsure how to answer her question. "Good. I've been busy. I'm leaving my new job already."

"Really? Where are you going?" Summer couldn't help but feel he was about to tell her something she didn't want to hear.

He looked away and took another bite of his toastie. Clearly, she was right. There was something he didn't want to say, so she waited patiently, coming up with all sorts of scenarios. Maybe he was ill. Maybe he'd met someone, which was fine. So had she. And Aaron deserved the best after what he'd been through with losing his mother. He chewed slowly, putting off swallowing his mouthful of toastie as long as he reasonably could get away with.

"Did I tell you I've met someone?" he said, eventually.

"No? But good. I'm happy for you. She better be amazing!"

"She is! Too good for me, really. She lives quite a bit away, though." He paused and looked at Summer for her reaction. She showed none. A stoical expression was easy now, thanks to having to listen to patient antics and show no obvious reaction.

"Where is quite a bit away?" she asked, taking another bite of food.

"Australia."

The piece of cheesy toast suddenly jammed in her throat. She gagged and coughed hard, luckily dislodging it pretty easily. Aaron laughed at her.

"Sorry! Didn't mean to shock you that much." He grinned.

"Australia? Aaron that's more than a bit away! I thought you meant London or something. Jeez."

"Yeah, I suppose it is about as far as you can get. But I'm so excited, Summer. Nurses can get visas apparently. And honestly, I think she's the best thing that ever happened to me."

"Visas? So, you're going to move there?" Summer put down her last piece of toastie, suddenly feeling full.

"Yep. Well, I'm going to try, anyway. They're quite strict on who can get a visa even with nurses."

"Oh, Aaron. I'm properly made up for you."

And though she meant every word, Summer couldn't help but feel a strong twinge of sadness that he would not be around anymore.

"Are you going to miss me?" he asked with a wink.

She shrugged. "Maybe a little."

"I bet Alex Swanson won't!"

Summer laughed. "What do you mean? He doesn't mind you at all."

"He puts up with me. There's a difference. Anyway, I'm glad I got to tell you in person. Wouldn't have been able to see you almost choke otherwise."

"Shut up!" Summer put the last piece of toastie in her mouth and grabbed a tissue to wipe her hands.

"So, what did you want to tell me?" he asked as he wiped his own hands, his face more serious now.

"Well, it's a strange one, to be honest," she began, not sure how to word her request.

"It's never *not* strange when it involves you, Summer."

Summer nodded. "Yes, you've got a point there. Anyway, I also might have a new job, working for the police as a forensic psychologist."

"Wowee, that sounds pretty cool!" Aaron whistled through his teeth.

"It sounds like it, but actually I've had my first taste of it this morning, and it's been tough." She lowered her voice. "A man claiming to be Andy Bailey's brother walked into the police station looking for me. He said Andy had told him I'm a spy for the police, and to talk to me about some ... some crimes he committed." It suddenly occurred to her that maybe she shouldn't be talking about this with Aaron. Too late now.

"Andy's brother?" Aaron's mouth dropped open, and her

heart sank. He clearly knew nothing about Billy Bailey either, then.

"That's what I thought. Andy doesn't have a brother from what I remember."

Aaron shook his head. "Andy Bailey does have one brother. He didn't know he had one until fairly recently. Something about being separated as kids. They were both in foster care, and they got split up. His brother found him a couple of years ago and arranged a visit to the hospital."

"Oh. What was he like? His brother?"

"The brother? No idea. I wasn't in whenever he visited. Actually, now that I think of it, I remember Izzy saying he was a bit weird. He didn't talk much. She said, 'Maybe schizophrenia runs in the family,' or something to that effect."

"Hmm. I'm trying to figure out if what he's said is true or not. It is quite extreme. Possibly a delusion, I guess."

"Well, what a great way to start your new job!"

"They haven't actually given me the job yet! This guy walked in right after my interview."

"So, a patient personally recommended you. That makes you look good right?"

Summer laughed again. "I'm not so sure. Depends how much trouble he gives my potential new boss, I guess."

A loud vibration shook the table and drew Summer's eyes towards her phone. Finally, Swanson was calling her. A ball of nerves suddenly crunched inside her stomach.

"Sorry, Aaron. This might be about Andy's brother. Do you mind?"

"No, you take the call." Aaron sat back in his chair and looked away as Summer answered the call.

"Summer, we've found a body. It looks like Billy is telling

the truth. But he probably won't tell us anything more without you." Swanson sounded even more strained than usual.

"Do you need me to come over to the station?" Summer asked.

"Not yet. We're going to talk to him first. Don't take that the wrong way. We just need to do everything by the book for if it goes to court. But we might need you later."

"OK. I'll keep an eye on my phone. Just let me know if you need me."

Swanson hung up without waiting for her to say goodbye. She put the phone down and looked at Aaron apologetically.

"I really have to go. I'm sort of 'on call.' Thank you for the toastie, and keep me updated on Australia. We can have a proper catch-up before you leave."

The pair stood, and Summer reached out to hug Aaron, suddenly wanting to tell him not to leave. She and Aaron may not have worked out romantically, but he was always there when she needed him. She sighed and let go, walking away with a sadness inside her that hadn't been there before. She gave him one last look as she walked through the exit, and he waved and gave her a sad smile. Despite what they'd said, she couldn't shake the feeling that this would be the last time she saw Aaron Walker.

Swanson

Within an hour, the house was swarming with officers and forensic teams. Swanson stood his ground in the back garden, but made sure he was far enough away to not bother the forensic guys. There was a white marquee, half hiding the area where the body lay. And they had confirmed it as a definite body. They found a hand first, followed by the torso, and they were now working on softly brushing away dirt to reveal the head.

Spying neighbours wouldn't be able to see anything, but Swanson could still see underneath the marquee from his spot. Hart was speaking to Gordon about the night the so-called animal dug up his garden, and whether he knew Billy Bailey or any missing people. He'd paled further since realising what was going on, and his son had since turned up to talk to Hart with him, which made Swanson feel a little better about what they were putting the poor guy through. Hart, Gordon and his son had retreated into the front living room forty-five minutes ago.

Swanson could see the body wore a mud-covered red coat, as he had guessed, and what appeared to be dark blue jeans. There were no shoes. Bare toes stuck out in an unnaturally twisted angle. Long, dark hair stuck to the red coat. At first glance it appeared to be a woman, just as Billy Bailey told them.

A wave of nausea hit Swanson as the all-too-familiar smell of rotting flesh reached him. He quickly held his breath and backed away until he was just outside of the open back door. They would send the body to the coroner's office as an urgent case, and hopefully have a report soon on her cause of death. Or maybe Billy would just tell them what happened. Asking him was worth a shot. Sharp footsteps came from behind, and he turned to see Hart walk into the kitchen.

"Get anything good?" he asked.

"Not much. He doesn't know Billy Bailey. He saw nothing six months ago and has no idea who the body might be. His son is looking after him, who has also never heard of Billy Bailey. Gordon's pretty shaken up. He's going to stay with his son tonight."

"Let's go talk to Billy, then," Swanson said. "He might have something to tell us."

"He isn't going to talk to us without Summer, is he?" Hart grumbled.

Swanson shrugged. "It's worth a shot."

Hart nodded reluctantly. They told Gordon they'd be back in touch and left him in peace with his red-faced son who seemed more stressed than Gordon himself. Out of habit, Swanson checked the side of his car for scratches before getting into the driver's seat, but there was nothing.

"It must be exhausting," Hart said as she clicked her seatbelt into place.

"What must be exhausting?" Swanson asked, only half listening as he pulled off the curb.

"Being so worried about your damn car all the time. Just get an old banger so you don't have to worry about it."

He ignored her and drove off towards the station. The clock on the centre console flashed 5:54 p.m. No wonder he had a headache after a day like today. Who wouldn't? And it was nowhere near over yet.

Before long, they arrived back at the station, and Marsh informed them on her way out that Billy Bailey had now been officially arrested on suspicion of murder.

"Thanks," Swanson said as Marsh left the station for the day. "Hart, want to go get him and I'll check over the interview room?"

"Fine," Hart mumbled and walked off towards the cell Billy was staying in.

Swanson waited in interview room one again, hoping that being in the same room would give Billy the sense of familiarity and trust that he needed to open up about the woman in the garden. It didn't take long for Hart to appear with Billy, and the smell of grease filled Swanson's nose once more. Still, it was better than the smell in poor Gordon Blacksmith's garden. Swanson said hello to Billy and introduced everybody in the room for the recording.

"We found the body, Billy," Swanson continued. "Thank you for cooperating and telling us where it was. Can you tell us who she is or what happened to her?"

Billy shook his head vehemently. "You said I could speak to Summer, and I won't say another word until she gets here."

"You can speak to Summer, Billy. But not right now. It's late. And you need to remember she isn't a police officer, despite what Andy says."

"I want Summer,"

"We could get you a legal representative," Hart offered in such a friendly manner that Swanson choked on his water.

"No."

Ten minutes later, Billy was still refusing to say a word other than to ask for Summer.

"OK, Billy. We'll see what we can do about getting Summer back, but I can't make any promises, and it's not likely to be today. It's already past seven o'clock." Swanson sighed.

"You already made a promise, and you should keep it," Billy replied, looking like a stubborn toddler who couldn't understand why he can't get his own way.

Hart brought Billy back to his cell, whilst Swanson stormed down to Murray's office, forgetting to knock in his frustration with Billy. She was sitting at her desk, and looked up at him with one eyebrow raised and her jaw set tight.

"He won't talk without Summer," he said in a clipped tone.

"She isn't trained, Swanson. This man is saying he murdered hundreds of people. He might be mentally ill, or it might be true. We know he's hurt one woman who's unconscious in hospital, and apparently murdered another. We need to make sure everything is legitimate here for when it gets to court."

"As long as I'm in there with her, it will be OK," Swanson insisted. "I'll make sure of it. She's basically his advocate, right? Because we're worried about his mental health. Her being there makes it more legitimate. We'll likely need an appropriate adult at some point."

Murray sighed. She rubbed her eyes before looking back up at Swanson. "Fine. But not until tomorrow. And be aware, if this goes wrong, you could lose your job, because I'm not putting my ass on the line."

Swanson

Swanson cursed as the sunlight seeped into the living room of his Ockbrook cottage the next morning, and he realised he'd fallen asleep on the sofa again. Like usual, he was fully dressed. At some point he had curled up to rest his head for five minutes and conked out completely. At least this time he had taken off his work suit, and had slept in tracksuit bottoms and a gym T-shirt instead. There was nothing worse than waking up on the sofa in yesterday's crumpled suit.

He stretched out, attempting to ease the cramp in his lower back and wondering if it was normal to fall asleep so quickly on the sofa. He remembered looking at his phone last night and thinking about how to reply to a text from Summer asking if he was still going over to her flat at 9pm. *Oh no, Summer!* Had he even replied?

He sat up straight and stretched again as he looked around for his phone. Eventually he found it buried underneath a cushion behind his head. He hadn't replied to Summer. Great. She'd be pleased with him today. He opened her last text message.

'If you're not coming over, what time do you want me to come and see Billy tomorrow?'

He checked the time – it was 6:15 a.m. Probably a little too early, even for a morning person like Summer. He started writing a reply – *'Maybe 9:00 a.m.?'* When another text appeared; this time from Hart.

'She's awake. Let's go.'

He stared at the text for far too long before realising she must mean Marcie. Marcie Livingstone was awake. That was enough to get him to move. This could be the thing to make Billy talk.

He jumped up and rushed a shower and a slice of toast before throwing on yet another navy suit. The dark colours suited him; colourful patterns did not. Hart loved to jibe him about looking the same every day. Plain but smart – exactly how he liked it. He texted Summer to let her know it would be around 11:00 a.m. before they got to interview Billy again.

By 8:00 a.m., the harsh smell of hospital disinfectant and illness crept up Swanson's nostrils and clung like a sticky residue. He wrinkled his nose and continued through the busy corridors of Derby Hospital. He snaked past preoccupied doctors, overly jovial porters pushing vast beds and busy nurses with well-earned black bags under their tired eyes.

"I hate hospitals," he muttered to Hart.

"Yes, Swanson, you tell me every time we visit one," she replied with a roll of her eyes. "Which is way too often. Normal people aren't in here this many times a month. Maybe you secretly love hospitals."

Swanson snorted. "It comes with the job. Plus, there was the brain tumour."

"Yes, but that's gone now so stop milking it. And we do seem to be here a lot even so!" she insisted.

It wasn't long before they reached the ward where doctors had placed Marcie Livingstone. She'd been very lucky. The doctor had agreed to her being interviewed because her injuries were not as bad as first thought, save some superficial damage to her face and head. Though they were keeping her in for now to make sure.

Swanson pushed the buzzer on the outside of the ward door. He wrinkled his nose one last time before forcing his face into its usual stoical expression. The sour medicinal smell made his stomach clench, a reminder of the frequent hospital visits for his own health in the past year.

"Seems like she was quite lucky considering Billy hit her in the face so hard," Hart mused as they waited for a nurse to buzz them into the ward.

"She was lucky they were interrupted," Swanson reminded her.

The door in front of them made a short electric buzzing noise, and a junior nurse opened the door. She was a dark blonde with an upturned nose, and her cheeks dimpled when she grinned at them. Her gaze seemed to linger on Swanson, and he wondered why. He closed his lips and ran his tongue over his teeth to make sure nothing was stuck in them.

"Hi." Hart took the lead, also giving Swanson a strange glance. "We're here to see Marcie Livingstone. Is she on this ward?"

"Hi, yes! I was told you'd be coming." She stepped to one side to allow them inside. Swanson noted her name tag said 'Daisy.' "Marcie is in one of the side rooms. I'll take you through and make sure she's OK to talk to you."

Swanson followed Daisy through the ward, smiling politely at passing nurses and their assistants, who paused to take notice of him and Hart. Near the end of the ward were three private rooms. Daisy walked up to the middle room and turned to them.

"Give me a sec. I'll just make sure she's OK before letting you in," she explained.

Swanson nodded and turned to look through the other room. The bed was just visible through the open door. A beautiful young woman lay in it, her eyes closed. Her skin was white with a sheen of sweat, and dark hair stuck to her forehead. Guilt tore his gaze away just as Daisy reappeared.

"She's happy to talk to you. Don't be too long, though, please. She's very lucky, but she needs to rest." She looked at both of them in turn with a stern glare and rushed off to tend to other patients.

He waved a hand at Hart. "After you."

Hart nodded and made a concentrated effort to soften her face with a friendly smile. She didn't do it often, but looked disturbingly sweet when she made the effort. He stayed behind her as they entered the ward. The last thing Marcie needed was a hairy, oversized man looming over her whilst she was recovering from an attempted murder.

The private room was small, and the only things that fit in were the bed and a bedside table, along with some beeping medical equipment on the other side. A TV on a movable arm hung above the bed. Marcie was propped up in bed by plumped pillows.

Pale hands lay clasped in her lap, and curly black hair fell limply around her shoulders. She gave them a small smile, her head hanging slightly so hair partially covered one side of her face. But it didn't fully hide the large gauze above her left eye, or the angry, red bruising around her cheek. The edges of which were creeping into a purple shade.

"Hi, Marcie," Hart said. "I'm Detective Inspector Rebecca

Hart, and this is my colleague, Detective Inspector Alex Swanson."

Swanson nodded in greeting. He noticed Marcie's clasped knuckles were whiter than the rest of her pale skin. She seemed scared. A jolt of sympathy ran through him, followed swiftly by anger at Billy.

"We're here to ask you a few questions about what happened to you, is that OK?" Hart continued.

"Yes. Thank you for coming." Marcie's soft voice shook a little as she spoke, and she cleared her throat as if to get rid of her nerves.

"Great, thank you." Hart nodded towards a couple of white, plastic chairs next to the bed. "Do you mind if we take a seat?"

Marcie shook her head delicately. She was just a kid, really. Early twenties at the most, and as Swanson moved to her other side to squish into one of the bloody awful chairs, the uninjured part of her oval-shaped face became more visible. Her eyes were bright blue behind the bruising, and she watched them intently as they sat down.

"How are you feeling?" Hart asked her with a sympathetic smile.

"A bit sore." Marcie looked down, her lips suddenly set into a determined grimace. "But I'm just so glad to still be here that I don't care."

Hart nodded. "You've been through a lot. We'd just like you to walk us through what happened so we can catch who did this to you, if you feel able to, please."

Marcie looked back at Hart, her eyes wide. "I know who did this to me."

Hart raised an eyebrow. "Who was it?"

"My boyfriend. Billy Bailey." She paused and swallowed

hard, her eyes glistening. "He gets mad sometimes. It's like he's suddenly not himself. He's never hurt me this much before, though. He's not all bad."

Swanson's hand balled into a fist at the side of the chair. Hearing it in the station from Billy was one thing, but seeing the damage a so-called *man* did to her was much harder. Despite his feelings, his face did not belie his anger.

"Have you reported him for violence previously?" Hart asked.

Marcie shook her head. "I always hoped he would just stop and go back to how he used to be. But I do want to talk about this time." There was a flash of fire in Marcie's eyes. "I don't want to be with him anymore Not until he gets the help he needs."

"OK. And how long have you been with Billy?" Hart asked.

"About ten years. Since we were kids. We met at school."

Swanson's jaw clenched. Billy looked a lot older than Marcie, by at least ten years.

"OK, Marcie. He is actually in custody as we speak and he has admitted what he did to you. So, you are safe from him now. I just wanted to make sure that was what happened. If you can please talk me through what he did?" Hart asked.

Marcie nodded and tucked her hair behind her ear, forgetting to hide the painful-looking marks on her face. Fresh blood marked the white gauze, and the bruising was angrier than Swanson first thought. "It's a bit blurry but I'll try my best. We were at home. I think we were eating dinner. And then I suddenly felt" – she paused as she searched for the right word – "ill."

"Ill in what way?" Hart prompted further.

"Nauseous and dizzy. I must have passed out. When I came

to, everything was dark and I could barely breathe. There was something in my mouth, and I couldn't move my hands or arms." She swallowed hard again.

"What did you have for dinner?" Swanson asked.

Both women glanced at him as though they'd forgotten he was there. He shifted uncomfortably in his chair.

"Er, I don't know. I don't remember," she answered with a blank look.

"OK, please continue." Hart motioned with her hand.

"Well, like I said, everything was black and there was something on my face. I wriggled to get it off, and then fingers were clawing at my face and I think I screamed or shouted something. Then there was just pain." Her hands trembled as she spoke. "That's all I remember. But I know it was Billy."

"OK. Thank you, Marcie. We'll be in touch once we've spoken again to Billy. If he makes a full confession, you won't have to go to court. But if he denies it, we might need you in court. How do you feel about that?"

Marcie looked away. She sniffed as if holding back tears. "Will he get in trouble, or will he get help?"

Hart glanced at Swanson, both knowing how difficult it was to get help with mental illness through the prison system.

"A bit of both," Swanson answered as truthfully as he could. "Whether he goes straight to a mental health facility will depend on his actions, an evaluation by a psychiatrist and what happens in court."

Marcie nodded. "I'll do what's needed to get him help."

"Thank you, Marcie. We'll be in touch soon."

Swanson clenched his fists as they left the hospital ward. Talking to victims always ignited a fire in his chest, and he was going to make sure Billy paid handsomely for what he did to

Marcie Livingstone.

Summer

Summer picked up the last of the toys from the living room floor and threw them into the storage box beside the sofa, where Joshua had lain all morning looking pale.

"How are you feeling, baby?" She stroked her hand across his sweaty forehead.

"Not good," he mumbled, not taking his eyes off the TV. "And I'm seven now, Mummy. I'm not a baby."

She sighed and checked her phone to see if his dad, Richard, had replied about picking him up – nothing. And if she didn't go into the station because of childcare issues now, no way was she getting the job. Thank god for her mother.

"Are you well enough to go to Mamma's?" she asked.

"I suppose so," he said in a quiet voice which pulled at Summer's guilty heart strings. She kissed him on the forehead and went to the kitchen to call her mother, who agreed to have him without hesitation.

An hour later she'd dropped him at her mother's house in Ilkeston and was pulling into the station, trying to put the guilt out of her mind. This job would be three days a week, and the same pay as her full-time advocacy job. If she could get through today, it would be well worth it to be around more for him.

It was 10:00 a.m. by the time she reached the station. Murray stood on the steps waiting for her, as promised because of Summer not having a staff card. Murray looked immaculate as usual in a light-blue trouser suit and hair pulled back into a perfect bun.

"Morning, Summer." Murray gave her a momentary smile but didn't wait for a response as she opened the door and waved Summer through. "Thanks for coming back. Swanson and Hart are on their way back from the hospital. You'll be interviewing Billy Bailey with a different officer, Lisa Trent. She said you've met."

"Er, yes. Briefly." Summer thought back to the intimidating woman she'd bumped into yesterday.

"Great. Meet her in interview room one. Grab yourself a drink first if you want one, and I'll be in my office if you need me. Trent can explain everything else regarding the interview."

Summer nodded and Murray walked off. She grabbed a glass of water from the empty kitchen and ignored the sick feeling in her stomach as she approached the door to the interview room. It was closed, and though it felt wrong to be wandering around the police station alone, she gently pushed it open.

To her surprise, Billy was already in the interview room, staring down at the table, and DI Trent was sitting across from him. Trent startled at the door opening and stopped talking, as if Summer had interrupted her from getting some information. Summer hesitated in the open doorway, her mouth partly open but unsure what to say.

Trent gave her a quick smile, however, and nodded at the chair next to her. Billy looked up and watched her as she sat and got comfortable in the chair. He didn't blink. Summer felt his stare on her the whole time.

"Hello, Billy," Summer said in a calm voice. She smiled at him. Although he'd requested to speak to her, he didn't smile back or act warm towards her at all. He simply continued to stare, which was at least more than he would do for any police officers. "How are you doing?" she asked.

"I want to see Marcie," he replied. His voice was eerily soft and childlike. Not the voice of a killer. It gave Summer a weird chill.

"Do you think she will want to see you?" Trent asked, one eyebrow raised in surprise.

His eyes shot across to Trent, and he finally blinked. Summer felt a wave of relief on his behalf, and on hers that he was no longer staring at her.

"I wasn't talking to you," he said to Trent, who raised both hands and sat back in her chair, turning expectantly to Summer.

"Well, do you think she'd want to see you?" Summer repeated Trent's question, intrigued to know the answer. She knew what hers would be if a man had just tried to murder her.

"Yes, of course. She loves me." He huffed and looked back down at the table. "How is she?"

"I'll find out soon, and then we can discuss seeing her, OK?" Summer could use this as leverage. She pondered for a moment how best to bribe him without it being too obvious. She gave Trent a sideways glance, unsure if she expected Summer to lead the enquiry. It would have been much easier if Trent had waited to interview Billy so they could've had a chat beforehand.

"We found the body of a young woman at the address you gave us," Trent said. "Can you tell us who she is?"

95

He shook his head.

"Do you know her name, Billy?" Summer asked.

"Not her full name. She told me her name was Ciara."

"What were you doing in Long Eaton at that time?" Summer tried.

"I needed a place to stay. I was in a flat across the road from that house but needed to get out. I knew the owner's car hadn't been there for a few days, so I climbed over his fence and slept in his shed for a few nights."

"And how did you meet the woman?"

"I went for a few drinks in Long Eaton, met her at the bar. We got talking, and she wanted to come back to my flat. I tried to pretend like I lost my keys, but she started freaking out, and then she called me some horrible names. I picked up a rock and hit her round the head. She was dead within seconds."

He shook his head as if name calling was far worse than anything he'd done. The actions of this guy seriously suggested some type of personality disorder.

"Do you remember what she looked like?" Trent butted in.

He pursed his lips for a moment, deep in thought. "Longish brown hair, tanned skin. She wore a red coat. I think she had black boots on, too."

"Thanks, Billy. We should be able to identify her from that information," Trent replied. "Let's take a quick break."

Trent stood and motioned for Summer to follow her. Outside the interview room, she whipped out her phone and closed the door.

"Murray, these are the details of the woman. Missing from a bar in Long Eaton, first name Ciara, brown hair, white with tanned skin, wearing a red coat and black boots when she disappeared."

She uttered some quiet replies whilst Summer stood looking at her, awkwardly leaning against the wall and wondering what to do next. Trent put her phone down and sighed before raising one hand and running it across her face and hair.

"What did Murray say?" Summer asked.

"She's going to ask someone to look into it. As long as this woman was reported missing, it shouldn't take long at all to find who it was."

A sudden thought occurred to Summer. "I remember a woman going missing from Long Eaton six months ago." She got out her own phone and brought up the search engine.

"Do you? What was her name?"

"I'm just looking for it now. It was big news at the time. My mum lives in Ilkeston, and it's the same borough." Summer scrolled furiously through news articles looking for the name. "Aha, here it is. 'Forty-three-year-old mother of two, Ciara Dempsey, disappears from Long Eaton night out.'"

Trent grabbed the phone from Summer and read through the article herself. "Well, bingo. I guess we've found Ciara Dempsey."

The Trio - 21 Years Before

Mrs Silly Tilly loomed over the bed, rolling pin still in her hand. The pain in my back and legs was even worse than the time I broke my arm, but I didn't cry. I stared at her and held my breath to stop the tears from coming. A week had passed, but she didn't look the same anymore. That stupid old lady hairstyle was a wig, and she took it off as soon as Nadene and Ben disappeared. She wore jeans and a tight top and walked around in the same big shoes my mum used to wear when she was going out somewhere.

And she didn't bake. Lauren told me the apple pie was from the local farm shop.

"What do you do next time I tell you to run me a bath?" she asked in a low voice. At least she'd stopped shouting. Though her low voice was worse sometimes. I took a breath to make sure my voice didn't shake. At least I knew the answer this time and wouldn't get another whack with the pin.

"Run you a bath," I replied.

It turned out I was wrong. The pin came down hard on my leg once more. I cried out, unable to stop the burst of tears.

"Run you a bath, what?" she asked in the same calm voice.

"Ma!" I cried. "Run you a bath, Ma!"

I can't believe I was stupid enough to forget to call her Ma.

Ma. Ma. Ma. I needed to say it after every sentence.

"That's right, and why do you call me Ma?" she asked.

I gulped, trying to make the big lump in my throat go away. It was bigger than the time I fell over in front of everyone at Becky Marsdens birthday party. Not as big as when my parents died though.

"Because I'm yours now."

"Yes. You live here now. There is no getting away. There's no more Nadene. No more Ben. No more family. This is your life. You are mine. You do your chores. You eat. You go to bed. Do you understand?"

I nodded, unable to make the lump any smaller to speak again.

But suddenly my hair felt tight, and I cried out again in pain. She'd grabbed me by my hair and yanked me up. I closed my eyes, but felt her breath on my ear.

"Don't ever fucking disobey me again," she growled, almost like an animal.

"I won't, Ma!" I cried out.

She leaned forward, her lips right to my ear. "I know what you did, little girl."

My heart dropped to my stomach as though she'd packed it with lead.

"I know what you did to your poor parents, and I'll make sure you pay for it."

I didn't respond. How could she know? All I could think about was the pain in my head as she yanked my hair even tighter. There was no point trying to argue.

"That's why Nadene sent you here, see? All three of you are fucking broken, and it's my job to make you upstanding members of the community. So do not disobey me again."

She let go of my hair, and I fell to the bed. Her footsteps faded away as she left the tiny bedroom we shared. Through the still darkness, I tried to stop the tears from coming, but they came out anyway. I rubbed the pain on my legs and tried to reach my back. They both throbbed. I was definitely going to have the biggest bruise ever tomorrow. I closed my eyes and tried to pull over the scratchy blanket. Then I heard a creak from one of the other beds, and footsteps getting closer. A soft hand stroked my head, and a body longer than mine climbed into bed next to me.

"Lauren?" A little voice called out quietly in the darkness, barely more than a whisper. "Can I come?"

"Yes, Billy," replied Lauren. "Come on. Sneak, though."

A pitter patter of little feet thudded softly over the carpet, and another small body was suddenly on the other side of me. He was kind of leaning on my bruises, but I didn't mind. Billy wasn't as annoying as I thought he'd be.

"It will be OK," Lauren whispered. "We got you."

The lump in my throat finally lessened. And I closed my eyes as the weight of little Billy somehow made me feel safer, and Lauren stroked my head just like my mum used to when I'd grazed my knee. And somehow I knew, it would be OK. I would survive this. We'd survive together. The trio.

Summer

"And you've admitted that you committed other murders?" Summer asked, back in the room with Billy and Trent.

He nodded.

"Can you tell me about these?" Summer asked.

He shrugged. Summer inhaled and swallowed down the urge to shake him by his shoulders. His motivation was still unclear to her. Both the motivation to kill and the motivation to confess. A lot of criminals who end up confessing either feel guilt or want fame and recognition. Billy didn't seem to feel guilty or like he wanted any recognition. Marcie was the only motivator here.

"How about you tell us some more about these murders, and where the bodies are? And by the time you finish, I should be able to check on Marcie for you," Summer tried again.

"Yes, OK. It can be hard for me to remember, but I'll try. There were definitely a few in the woods near my old house. I woke up there a few times, and the path I used to take was always something that stuck in my head."

"And where's that?" Trent asked, her hand poised over her notepad.

"Bell Woods, in Ilkeston. From the entrance, walk straight

for one mile." He paused and looked away as if deep in thought. "Then turn right, and two hundred forty-six steps later there's a clearing."

Summer felt sick to her stomach. Bell Woods was where she played as a child. Her friend had accidentally smashed a bus stop just outside it by absentmindedly sling shotting stones one day, and they'd ran inside the woods fearing arrest. They'd copied the easiest *Jackass* movies and filmed them on the first ever flip phones with cameras, and built a colossal tree house one summer so they could get drunk inside with no adults seeing. It was where she had her first taste of a disgusting warm can of beer at thirteen years old and then spat it back out all over the tall boy who bought it for her: James Evans. He'd run away a few years after that. She felt Trent glancing at her, but she didn't speak.

"What is there?" Trent continued scribbling furiously, but he didn't respond.

"Billy? Who's there?" Summer repeated.

"Two women, I think. And a boy. A young boy."

Summer's stomach lurched as she thought about her own young son. "How young?"

He shrugged. "Maybe seventeen or so."

"What were their names?" Summer asked.

He let out a snort through his teeth. "It was a long time ago. I've no idea," he said, as though it were a ridiculous question. Summer glanced at Trent, who was still making notes.

"How long ago?" Summer asked instead.

"About two years since the last one, I reckon." He paused. "Actually, one of them was called Cara. I remember her, Cara Percy."

"And who was Cara?" Trent asked.

Billy sighed loudly. "I need a break now."

"You'll get one soon. Tell me who Cara is, please?" Trent asked again.

"She was just a girl. No one special."

"Then why did you kill her?" asked Summer.

He looked back at Summer, his cold eyes unblinking once again. "Because I wanted to."

Summer showed no reaction, despite her body tensing up. "And why did you want to kill her, Billy?"

"She was nasty." He spat the last word as if it was poison. "I found her on a night out, drunk on god knows what. She was half naked and puking her guts up. She called me a homeless tramp after I offered to help her. I did her family a favour. She was an embarrassment to them."

OK. Now she was getting somewhere. His story reminded Summer of a previous patient she'd worked with who kept attacking women he thought looked down on him. "It sounds like she was very rude." She felt Trent glance at her, but she continued. "What exactly did you do to make her pay?"

"She was rude." He nodded, as if vindicated. "I found a bottle in an alleyway and smashed it around her head."

"You remember it clearly, then?" Trent asked. "What did it feel like?

A flash of panic crossed his face – the only emotion he'd shown since talking about the murders.

"What do you mean?" he asked.

"What did it feel like to smash that bottle across her head?" Trent asked, her eyes hard.

"I n-need a break," Billy stammered.

"No problem. You can take a break as soon as you've answered my question," Trent replied.

"No. I need a break now. I need a drink, too."

Trent sighed and crossed her arms, leaning back in the chair. She stared at Billy, and for a moment Summer thought she was going to refuse his request for a break. But after a few seconds, she shifted in her chair and ended the recording.

"Come with me, please, Billy. I'll be back in a moment, Summer."

She returned a few minutes later nervously chewing her thumbnail. It was strange to see someone as intimidating as Trent chew her nails. She sat back down next to Summer and lowered her hand before giving Summer a quizzical look.

"I don't trust him," she said. "There's something off about him."

Summer nodded slowly. "Me neither. There's something I can't put my finger on, but at least he's talking."

"Yes. We need to check out Bell Woods. I'm going to ring Hart and see where she is." She stood to leave, but she stopped midway across the room. She looked at the ground and chewed her lip.

"Are you OK?" Summer asked.

"Yes, fine. I just remembered Swanson is more likely to answer than Hart. I'll call him." She flashed a smile and turned to leave the room.

"OK," Summer called out to her back. "I'll speak to Murray, then."

Trent stopped in the doorway. "No, don't bother. I'll see her now."

She walked off so quickly that Summer didn't have a chance to reply, and she was left with no idea what to do next. She considered how long it might take Billy to want to talk again, and the guilt of not being with Joshua pulled at her once more.

Hearing about the lives Billy took far too soon made the guilt even worse. She whipped out her phone and video called her mother.

"How is he?" she asked once her mother's pale face appeared on screen. Her mother always looked frail – mainly from years of alcohol abuse after Dad died.

"See for yourself," her mother replied and moved away from the camera. She pointed it at Joshua. "Mummy's calling, Joshie."

"Hi, Mummy!" Joshua yelled. He stood in the middle of the living room. "Look, see what I can do!"

He stood in a pose reminiscent of a ninja with two hands up in front of chest. Then he ran at the sofa yelling something like 'hiyah.' He kicked into the air before careening into the sofa and laughing hysterically.

"Wow, amazing! Watch Mamma's sofa, though."

"No, no. He's fine," her mother called out from behind the phone. Though she definitely would have punished Summer for doing that as a child.

"You're feeling better, then?" Summer asked him, the guilt dissolving somewhat at seeing his joy.

"What? Yeah, I'm fine, Mummy," he replied, as if she was nuts for asking.

He'd long forgotten this morning's illness, and as Summer looked at him and heard her mother's laugh, she realised where she needed to be after hearing Billy's repulsive confession. Though her heart sank as she realised maybe Murray was right. Maybe she wasn't cut out for this job after all.

Swanson

Bell Woods was an area covering a meagre one hundred acres of the land between the old mining town of Ilkeston and the small village of Horsley. Swanson knew the area a little from previous walks around the Derbyshire countryside, but he'd never been inside Bell Woods. He was curious what it would be like. Probably nothing like the rolling hills of the awe-inspiring Peak District. Small-scale woods can't give the same mental exhilaration as climbing something like Kinder Scout or a nice waterfall.

Summer's mum lived in Ilkeston close to the woods, and Swanson noted Summer's car parked on the road outside as he drove past. For a second, it tempted him to pull over and forget about the possible dead bodies buried nearby. He didn't have to go looking for bodies. He could just quit his job. He could grab Summer and go for a relaxing walk and meet Joshua.

But he knew that would never happen. At least this way he could do something to make his life worthwhile. And there was something in him that would never allow him to stop without feeling tremendous guilt.

"There's Summer's mum's house," Hart pointed out, having visited the house once when Summer thought her mother was in danger.

"Yes," replied Swanson, not sure what else to say.

"You could visit your future mother-in-law. She'd love that."

He gave her a look similar to the one a parent might give a silly child, and she laughed loudly.

"Summer's car is there, too." She pointed at Summer's blue BMW. "I thought she was back at the station."

"So did I," Swanson replied, making a mental note to check on Summer and make sure she was OK.

He pulled out onto the main road where the entrance to the woods was situated. There was a low wall, with a tight bundle of tall trees behind it and a small gap to drive through in the middle. Swanson saw a sign welcoming you to Bell Woods, but it wasn't visible from the road. If you didn't know about Bell Woods from a local, or from being a walker, you'd never think it was an actual road you were allowed to drive on.

As he drove inside, the light dimmed, and it pleased him to see there was no enormous car park or grand entrance. Wild trees hung over the road and blocked the cloudy sky with their ancient branches. There was a natural opening to the right-hand side, but it was only enough room for about four cars to park. No other cars currently made use of the space, which was fine with Swanson. It was easy to see why someone would think it a good place to bury a body – or several bodies.

"This place is a mood," Hart muttered as they got out of his car.

Swanson stopped dead and stared at her, one foot still in the doorway. "This place is a mood? What does that even mean?"

"I mean, if someone asked me, 'What does Swanson's usual vibe consist of?' I'd tell them to look at this place. Then they'd understand the moodiness I put up with."

She smiled sweetly at him as he glowered and pulled open

the boot of his car.

"I heard someone saying it on TikTok, and I quite like it. I'm not old before my time like you, Swanson. We're only in our thirties, you know. We're not ancient."

"I am not dignifying that statement by continuing this conversation. You might not be old, but you are too old for TikTok. Here." He passed her an empty evidence bag and some plastic shoe covers.

"It's addictive." She took the bags and shoved them into her winter coat pocket.

"Don't know why you're wearing that big coat. It's nearly twenty degrees." He shook his head in disgust.

"It isn't twenty degrees, though, is it? It's not even seventeen and clearly about to rain." She pointed up to the grey clouds that had gathered overhead. Swanson had to admit it was cooler than the previous day, at least.

They ambled into the woods side by side, Swanson with his phone held out to tell them when they'd walked a mile. After the initial wildness of the woods, it disappointed him to see a neat, concrete path spreading through the middle, which darkened his mood even further. There was no point in ruining natural beauty just to make an area easier to walk through. It was supposed to be hard to walk through.

This one even had a small wooden fence on either side of the path, with the odd gap to allow walkers in and out of the trees. He wondered if Joshua enjoyed walking. It'd be nice to take him and Summer out through the Peak District hills. Maybe even up Kinder Scout. He racked his brain to think about whether he'd seen children up there. He'd definitely seen them up Mam Tor. Maybe they could go there.

"Keep going straight for one mile. Is that what Trent said?"

Hart's voice brought him back to the present.

"That's what she said. Then turn right."

They didn't speak again as they trod down the concrete path, each lost in their own thoughts. It crossed Swanson's mind how unusual it was for Hart to be so quiet, but knowing her extreme dislike of anything related to the outdoors, it was likely their surroundings.

The last of the summer's charming rhododendrons swayed in the eerie breeze that whistled through the branches, spotted with pretty brambles and juicy-looking blackberries. But even the pretty scenery couldn't shake the loneliness of the dull woods. The ancient trees were so wide either side of the path that their branches met in the sky, blocking out natural light and warmth from above. Hart had the right idea with her big coat, not that he'd admit that to her.

They passed no one, other than one couple holding hands and glancing over at them with wary looks – probably because of Swanson looking exactly like a DI in his dark suit. He checked the distance on his phone and realised they'd just gone past the one-mile mark. He stopped and put a hand out to Hart, who froze mid-step. She followed him without a word as he took a few steps back.

"Here." Swanson pointed right. There was no gap in the little wooden fence here. He walked forward and climbed over it easily, looking back to make sure Hart could climb over. But even she could cock her leg over the pointless fence with ease.

"Let's go right then, I guess. I'll count. You have giant footsteps." Hart bent down to place the plastic bags over her shoes.

There was no longer any path, and broken branches hidden by piles of dried leaves covered the ground underfoot. Thorny nettles grabbed at their legs, and unseen critters scrambled to safety around them as they heard their footsteps approach.

"Two hundred and forty. Only six more steps to go," Hart said.

Sure enough, the trees opened up to a small, circular clearing, and a familiar adrenaline ran through Swanson. This place knew death. The air was thick with sorrow. He sniffed and wrinkled his nose. The all-too-familiar smell of rotten flesh lingered faintly in the fresh air. He moved forward and scoured the ground, but there were no obvious burial places in the clearing.

"Could be anywhere round here really, couldn't it?" Hart moaned.

Swanson was tempted to dig anywhere, but took a stroll around the clearing to search for some sort of clue. The ground was covered in the same bark and stems as the rest of the walk since they came off path. He gently kicked the debris around, but any specific burial areas were long gone over the years.

"Did you know this part of the soil structure on the top of the forest floor is called the O horizon?" Swanson asked, aware that it sounded boring, but he'd actually been fascinated while reading about it one day. The way the dead vegetation sustains new life. Or dead bodies, possibly, in this case.

"No, Swanson. I find that absolutely amazing, though. Thank you."

She rolled her eyes and continued to stare around the floor. The dull sun flashed through the clouds and glinted on an object across the way from where he stood. He frowned and walked over to it.

"Here," he called over his shoulder to Hart, who had been about to sit down on a rock.

"What is it?" she asked.

"Look here. This is weird."

Swanson pointed to a set of large rocks which were mostly buried in the dry mud. Someone had arranged them in a circle, and within the circle were three smaller rocks.

"Did he mention anything about a sign?" Hart asked.

"Trent didn't say anything... It's probably worth a look though?" Swanson tugged in his beard as he studied the rocks. "I can't see any other signs around here."

He snapped a picture of the rocks before digging his shovel softly into the ground, careful not to go too deep for fear of disturbing any weak bones or evidence. After twenty minutes, his shovel came across a blockage. He used his gloved hand to brush away remaining mud and soil, and something soft caught his attention. Swanson sighed and closed his eyes. He'd really been hoping Billy Bailey was simply mentally ill and had actually only murdered once. But it was becoming more and more apparent that he was telling the truth.

"What is it?" she asked.

He looked up at her, his face grim. "Dark cloth. It might be nothing, but we'd better get forensics in just in case."

Hart nodded and pulled out her phone. She walked away to call forensics, and Swanson gently fiddled with the dark cloth. There was something solid within it – a bone, maybe? His stomach lurched. Dead bodies were not something he'd ever gotten used to, and he already knew his dreams would be dark for a while. It would be some time before he made it off the sofa and into bed.

"They'll be here within an hour," Hart called across the clearing. Her own face looked a little pale. "I'll go to the car park to meet them, unless you'd rather?"

As tempted as he was to say he'd go to the car park, he couldn't let Hart stay here alone with possibly three dead bodies. "You go," he replied.

She nodded and turned to walk away. Swanson took more pictures of the mud and the cloth, making sure he got pictures of the clearing itself, too. His phone buzzed, and he almost ignored it, but Hart's name flashed up.

"Yes?" he answered.

"Hey, don't shoot the messenger, OK?" she said in a nervous voice. More nervous than he'd ever heard her. And Hart didn't get nervous often. His heart immediately froze.

"What is it, Hart?"

"It's your car—"

"My car? What the hell is wrong with my car?" Swanson started walking immediately.

"Are you walking? I can hear you walking! Stop right there. You can't leave the scene yet."

Swanson forced his feet to stop. "What is wrong with my car, Hart?" he asked again through gritted teeth.

"There's a note on it."

"Just a note? Jeez, Hart. Maybe lead with that next time." He put one hand on his chest to calm his heart. "What does it say?"

"It says, *'Billy isn't your guy.'*"

"So, someone is saying Billy is lying? Some random person is now the killer and someone's left a note on my car?" His headache suddenly reappeared with much more intensity than yesterday.

"Yes, and that someone clearly followed us here. Or knows where and who you are, at least."

His heart lurched. That same someone could be watching

Hart right now, and she was alone. "OK. Come back to me right now. We can wait here together just in case they're still around." He eyed the surrounding trees cautiously but saw nothing out of the ordinary.

"I'm already on my way. There's something else—" Hart cleared her throat as if scared to say what it was.

"Yes, Hart? Spit it out. It can't be that bad."

"They also smashed your car windscreen."

Summer

Summer picked Swanson up from the Audi garage at 6:00 p.m. She smiled sympathetically at him as he got into the passenger seat. Though she was wary of his mood knowing how particular he was about his car. It occurred to her she had never really seen him angry. Grumpy, yes. Often. But never angry. But he looked no more miserable than usual as he clicked his seatbelt into place.

"How bad is it?" she asked with a wince.

"It's just a new windscreen, luckily. No other damage done," he replied, though his tone of voice was definitely more clipped than usual. He may have been more annoyed than he looked.

"Here." She passed him a brown paper bag and set off toward Ockbrook, where his cottage was situated at the top of a hill. Which was fitting for someone who loved hills so much. Summer couldn't think of anything worse than climbing up those damn peaks in the countryside. And for no reason other than to look at a view she could easily just look at pictures of.

"What's this?" he asked, taking the bag and peeking through an open corner.

"Pull it open and see. It's just a little something to cheer you up."

The smell of meat and pastry came out when he pulled apart

the bag. He reached in and pulled out a large slab of pork pie, grinning as he turned to her.

"Pork pie? You really know how to cheer a man up." He placed the pie back into the bag.

"There's more." Summer nodded towards the paper bag and tried to look casual. No need to be nervous. If he said no, so be it. Swanson dug deeper inside the bag and pulled out a small piece of paper.

"A cinema ticket?" He read aloud the large writing on the rectangular note. It was clear someone had taken great care with each letter and tried to make them all very square and exactly the same size.

"Joshua made us all cinema tickets. He thought it would be nice if you came over to watch a movie." She swallowed down the nerves. "He likes to get the duvets out and all the cushions on the floor. We make loooots of snacks, too. It's fun. But don't feel you have to."

She risked a glance at his face, and out of the corner of her eye she swore she saw him smile. Or was it just wishful thinking?

"When for?" he asked.

"Well, we're going to do it tonight. But you don't have to come tonight. It can be done anytime. That's the beauty of home cinema!"

"I'd love to. Just not tonight." His smile dropped, and he turned away to look out of the passenger window.

Summer hid her disappointment by focusing on the road ahead. "That's OK. Don't worry about it."

"It's just work. When big things like this come in, anything else is impossible. It takes over my life. I need to focus on the case."

"Of course, you do. Have you had any updates from

forensics?" Summer asked in a more business-like tone.

"No, but Hart might have. I'll call her when I get home. My phone's dead at the minute. Did anything else happen on your end?"

"Nothing. He's refusing to speak to me now unless he speaks to Marcie. Trent called her, but she refused. She was terrified of talking to him again."

"I don't blame her."

"I'm going to try again tomorrow once we know what forensics found and I've got something to give him. I just don't get him. He doesn't seem to be motivated by fame or recognition. He doesn't feel remorse."

"He's a strange case alright." Swanson scratched at his beard, and then turned to Summer. "Do you believe him?"

Summer chewed her lip. "Do I believe him? That's a strange question. He said he did it, and he told us where the bodies are. Marcie confirmed it was him who attacked her. What's not to believe?"

"I don't know. Someone left a note on my car, but I didn't mention it. I'm guessing it was the same person who smashed my windscreen."

"A note? What did it say?"

"Basically, he's a liar and someone else is the murderer."

"What?" Summer's mouth fell open. "I have had the feeling there's something strange about what he's saying – other than the obvious horror of his actions. But why would he lie?"

Swanson shrugged. "I'd suggest the attention, but he doesn't seem to want any."

Summer whistled through her teeth. "So, someone knows something, and they want to make sure you know there's more to the story."

"Or, the person who left the note is the actual killer."

Summer swerved off the A52 leading to Ockbrook. "You really think so?"

"It's possible. Now they want recognition, but they want me to hunt for them first."

"Do you want me to ask Billy about it tomorrow?" Summer asked, wondering how to phrase it with him. This was really feeling out of her depth.

"Not yet. Let's save it for now."

Summer pulled up in front of Swanson's petite cottage, half hoping he'd invite her inside for a coffee; but also needing to get back to Joshua to relieve her mum of babysitting. She might love to have him, but the whole day was a long time for someone in her sixties who wasn't in the best of health.

"Thanks for the lift." He nodded at her and opened his door.

"No problem," replied Summer, feeling deflated at his apparent lack of interest in inviting her inside. Despite the fact she probably would have refused.

"I'll see you tomorrow. Hart's picking me up in the morning, so I'll probably see you at the station if Billy's open to talking again."

He got out of the car, and she watched him walk up to his front gate. He turned and raised one hand to wave goodbye. She returned the gesture and watched him enter the cottage. She'd hoped to feel better about the day after seeing Swanson, but as she drove away, the feeling of wanting to walk away from the job increased tenfold.

She arrived at her mother's house just before 7:00 p.m. and pulled up on the road outside. She couldn't help but turn to look over at the main road, and in the distance, she could see the entrance to Bell Woods. Now instead of fond memories of daft teenage-hood, a chill ran up her spine.

She tried to look away, but a man crossing the road a couple of hundred feet away drew her attention. He was tall and dark. He looked familiar somehow. She watched him reach the other side of the pavement and head towards a side street opposite her mother's house. She knew that walk. His face came into view as he came closer, and a jolt of recognition hit her.

He was the father of James Evans, the teenager who ran away when they were kids. Well, James would have been about sixteen then. He looked older than his actual age, however, so he always brought beer and cigarettes for them because he could get served without ID. They'd all thought he ran away, at least. He always said he would run away when he was old enough to work. His dad was actually his stepdad, and he wasn't very nice to him since James's mum died of cancer when he was around eight years old. The man didn't beat James, but he shouted a lot and kicked him out sometimes for the silliest of reasons. He'd stayed on Summer's sofa one night when his dad wouldn't let him back inside because he went home ten minutes after his curfew.

She watched the man turn and walk off down the adjacent road. A nagging feeling tugged at her chest as she thought about James. She'd always been sad that he'd never contacted her or any of their other friends ever again. They were a close group at that point, and he wanted rid of his stepdad, not his friends. She looked over at Bell Woods again, Billy's words ringing in her ears.

"Two women, I think. And a boy. A young boy."

"How young?"

"Maybe seventeen or so."

Her heart sunk, but she thought about Billy. And she finally understood why Swanson and Hart kept going with this job. There was no chance she could walk away without knowing if James was buried in those woods. Even if it wasn't James, it was someone's friend, child or sibling. Now, she had the chance to help, too. And that wasn't something she was going to turn down.

Swanson

S wanson stretched out to relieve the ache in his back, reminding him once again that forty was only a few years away and sofas were no longer the best place to fall asleep. If they ever were. His eyes stung against the bright sunlight seeping in through the weak, pale-green curtains. He rubbed his eyes hard and gulped down the glass of water that lay on the floor beside him. His headache eased, and his thoughts cleared. The events of the previous day came to him, and he groaned thinking about his car and what forensics found in Bell Woods.

He pulled his bulk up with difficulty and scrambled around for his phone, finding it on the floor near his glass. At least he'd put it on charge before falling asleep. His eyes fell on the empty pizza box from last night, and the stale smell of meat and dough made his stomach turn. He stood and kicked it further away before opening up his phone. Three missed calls from Hart and one text message sent five minutes ago.

'They found two so far. One male and one female. On my way to pick you up, so I hope you're decent.'

Jesus. The body count was growing far too quickly. Who else had Billy killed? If it was Billy at all.

Though if he was lying, Swanson still couldn't figure out

why. Was he protecting someone? But then that person must not want to be protected if they're going round leaving notes on windscreens. None of it made sense. But it filled Swanson with determination to find out the damn truth behind who smashed his windscreen. Maybe Marcie would help if she was feeling better, though asking her to talk to Billy didn't sit right with him at all.

He cursed as he saw another missed call from Summer. *Was he supposed to go round last night?* He sent her a text to ask if she was OK and hoped she wouldn't be too annoyed that he hadn't called back.

An hour later Swanson was back at his peaceful desk, whilst Hart went to get herself some coffee from the corner shop, cursing the kitchen for running out. His phone buzzed and he looked down to see Trent's name pop up.

'Spoke to the family of Ciara Dempsey. Her partner and 17 yr old son were there. Sounds like it was her. Will catch up with you in a bit.'

He sighed and opened up his computer. He may as well focus on searching for details of the Cara Percy case, then. She'd disappeared two years ago following a night out. Interestingly, there had been an eyewitness: her best friend, Robin Jones. Robin saw the person who kidnapped Cara, but she'd had passed out, unable to save Cara. She believed someone had drugged them. Swanson knew someone had taken Billy's picture and fingerprints when he was charged. He checked his watch – 9:00 a.m. Perfect time to call Robin Jones and find out more.

He snatched up his phone and dialled the number saved for Robin Jones, praying she still used the same one. He hadn't changed his own phone number in about a decade. It rang out as he held his breath. At least that was a good sign. It continued to ring for what felt like an eternity, but as he was about to hang up, he heard a voice answer.

"Hello," he called. "Is this Robin Jones?"

"Who's asking?" a suspicious female voice replied in a rough tone.

"My name is Detective Inspector Alex Swanson—"

"Police?" she interrupted, sounding even more suspicious.

"Yes, Derbyshire police. I wondered if I could have a quick chat with you, if you're at home?"

Her heavy breathing was the only sound for a moment. He crossed his fingers that she wouldn't hang up. "About what?"

Swanson hesitated. He hadn't really wanted to bring it up via phone, seeing as it was such a traumatic experience. But it didn't sound like he was going to be able to see her otherwise.

"Well, just an old case I think you witnessed. I have some questions."

"About Cara?" her voice relaxed instantly. "Yes, absolutely. Are you looking into her again? Because it's about time somebody did something about it."

"Can I come round? It might better to discuss this face to face."

"No! No, you can't come round. I'm busy, and, well, my partner wouldn't like it, you see. But I can talk to you over the phone whilst he's out."

"Oh, OK. Well, I really just wanted to go over what you saw again, if you don't mind? It's always better to hear it from the horse's mouth."

She took a deep breath. "Sure. We went out to Derby and ended up at a club called RedNote. And we met some people. We were drunk and went back to their room for a party. Didn't know them – two women and a man. They seemed friendly enough." She paused, cleared her throat, then continued, "Stupidest thing we've ever done. They said they were from Notts and had rented a hotel room in Derby for the night, so we all drank in their hotel room. One girl went home after a while. Next thing I know, Cara's passed out. I tried to reach her to check on her, but my eyes were heavy and I couldn't keep them open. My whole body went limp. There was a mirror in front of me, and just when I closed my eyes, I saw Cara being picked up and taken away."

"By the man? Do you remember his name or what he looked like?"

"He said his name was James. He was small and skinny … kinda dirty looking if I'm honest. If he hadn't been with two women, we never would have trusted him."

"What happened to the other woman who was with him? The one who hadn't left already."

"I've no idea. Like I said, one disappeared pretty early on. The other stayed. She was pretty, had black hair. She had a tattoo on her left wrist that was like a strange little symbol."

"OK. How old do you think they might have been?"

"They looked about the same as us, so early thirties may—" She paused abruptly, and Swanson heard the noise of a closing door in the background. "I have to go. Sorry," she whispered, before hanging up the phone.

Swanson leaned back in his chair and placed the phone back down on his desk. The woman with a strange tattoo on her wrist might help them. If she was still alive, that is. He searched Cara Percy's file again, and hidden away inbetween the wrinkled sheets of paper he found a hand-drawn image of a strange, small tattoo. It had four lines in a square shape which didn't quite meet, and inside was a swirl of curved lines. It was certainly an unusual design. Or, at least not one he'd seen before. He took a screenshot and completed a Google image search, but nothing matching the symbol came up.

His phone buzzed, and he absentmindedly flicked his eyes over to the screen. What he read, however, made him jump out of his seat, his heart pumping fast.

'Your Audi is ready to be collected.'

Swanson

A light, summer rain pattered the car window as Swanson considered his next move. He brought the cool can of Fanta Lemon to his lips and watched people walk by him in the supermarket car park. He sighed. The sugary twang of lemon was so much better than the weird twang of tea. What was the obsession with tea in this damn country, anyway?

After taking him to the garage to collect his car, Hart had gone to the woods to find out what she could about the bodies. They'd now found a third body, which was female as expected, but they were searching for more nearby just in case. He considered going to meet her. She was expecting him, after all. But an idea played on his mind. One which Hart would definitely have a gripe with.

He checked his watch. It was now nearly 11 a.m. Early visiting hours in the hospital would end at lunchtime. *Bugger it.* He was only a few minutes away. He strapped in and put his foot down to reach the hospital, abandoning his car on a grass verge away from anyone else and hoping he wouldn't be inside long enough to get a ticket. The rain still landed softly as he walked across to the hospital entrance, and within fifteen minutes, the smell of the ward made his stomach turn once more. His hatred of hospitals had intensified thanks to the lingering memories of the previous year, and it didn't help that he was due a check-up soon. Maybe working on convicting a serial killer was a good enough excuse to delay the check-up. Not that Hart or Summer would allow that.

He hesitated at the entrance to the ward. Maybe he should have asked Hart to visit, or Trent. Hell, maybe even Summer would be better than him. He breathed through his mouth and ignored the waves of nausea as a hard-faced nurse on the ward delivered him to Marcie, who was now in the main ward rather than a private room. There were three beds on each side of the ward, with barely a few feet of space between them. Marcie lay in the end bed, close to the window. She still looked pale, and though bandages covered the ripped flesh, the surrounding bruising contrasted darkly with her pale skin. The nurse pulled the curtains around the bed and gave Swanson a stern look before she left them to it.

"Hi, Marcie." Swanson flashed his most charming smile, and she smiled shyly back at him. "How are you feeling?"

She nodded. "I'm feeling OK, considering. I might go home tomorrow."

"That's great news," replied Swanson, with more enthusiasm than his usual tone. He couldn't help but feel like he was talking to a child whilst around her. "I'm happy to hear you're doing OK. I came here to talk to you about something, though, if you don't mind?"

"Of course. I assume it's about the case against Billy?"

"Well, yes, and no. Billy has admitted to some pretty shocking past crimes, and he's staying in custody to talk to us about them. One in particular, involved a young woman. And I'm hoping you can help me identify who that young woman

126

was."

"Oh, I'll try." Marcie looked at him determinedly with her one good eye.

"So, all we know about her so far is that she had black hair, was pretty and in her late twenties or early thirties. She would have been out drinking with him in Derby two years ago, when he met two other women. They all went back to a hotel room together in Derby. They drugged one of the girls, and she woke up in the hotel room alone. The other girl disappeared, and we think we just found her body."

Marcie's face paled. Her mouth opened and she stuttered, but no words came out.

"Do you know who this woman might be? The one he was with," Swanson pressed.

She clamped her mouth shut and shook her head. Tears brimmed her eyes, but she closed them tightly.

"Sorry, but I suddenly don't feel well at all," she replied, her voice breaking.

Swanson didn't move. He kept his gaze focused on her. She knew something. It was written all over her terrified face. His eyes flicked to her left wrist, no tattoo.

"That's OK. Take your time. Please remember that you're a victim here, too."

She opened her eyes, which were still bloodshot, but she faltered with her mouth half open. It looked like she was going to cave and tell him what she knew, but she glanced away and shook her head again.

"Please, I really don't feel well. I need the nurse." She closed her eyes once more and turned away from him.

But every cylinder in Swanson's body was fired up. His nerves were on edge being so close to the information he could see was on the tip of her tongue.

"Marcie, please. Your information could really help us. It could help put him away. It could save somebody else from the pain you're suffering now."

"I need the nurse now, please." Her voice shook as she spoke.

He sighed inwardly, careful not to let his disappointment show too much. "Of course, Marcie. I'll get her."

Swanson stood and left the bedside to grab a nurse, avoiding the hard-faced one who didn't seem to like him much. Instead, he spoke to a friendly looking nurse to explain Marcie wasn't well and left the ward. Marcie couldn't be pushed too far. She needed time to think about whatever information she knew, and he needed to remain calm with her.

But once back in his car, he acted out his frustration on the Fanta Lemon can, eventually throwing the crushed metal into the rubbish bag he kept under the passenger seat. He shouldn't have gone in alone. What if he'd ruined their only shot at getting her to cooperate? If Billy had forced her into doing something, maybe she was too scared to say. Maybe Marcie would feel safer opening up to Hart. He grabbed his phone and texted her.

'Meet me at the station, I have an update.'

It didn't take long to receive her reply.

'Polite as usual, Swanson. Be there in 15.'

The Runaway - 19 Years Before

Today was the day. My tummy felt like knots were being tightened inside it but I said nothing to Lauren. I'd never seen her smile so much. Her face actually had some colour in it rather than being deathly pale. Billy was dressed in his boots that were a few sizes too big, but they should keep his feet warm. He was grinning like a maniac, but he said nothing. Billy didn't talk too much. Lauren did most of the talking.

"Have you got everything?" Lauren asked me in a low voice.

"I think so," I whispered back, the knots in my stomach getting tighter.

"OK. It's 5am so Ma won't be up for hours yet." She beamed like a thousand suns were in her tummy, not knots.

"Yep," Billy piped up, his face still serious. "But we need to be quiet sneaking downstairs."

"Of course, but we do that every morning don't we?" Lauren replied.

She walked over to the bedroom door and opened it slowly. She peeked her head around and looked left, then right. I could hear quiet snores floating across the hallway. She turned to us and nodded her head once. We followed her to the door as she opened it just slow as we did any other morning. It just felt more dangerous today.

She led the way out into the hallway, and down the stairs one at a time. We tried to walk at the same time as each other to lessen the noise, but the snoring never stopped. Once we reached the kitchen, I had to take really quick breaths to stop the knots in my stomach getting worse. I felt sick, but didn't want to ruin it for the others. Lauren reached out to the kitchen door handle, pulling it down just as slow as the bedroom door. But she said a really bad word under her breath. Billy's eyes widened. He'd never heard Lauren curse before. Ma would beat us if she heard us say any bad words. She turned to us, her eyes hard.

"It's locked. Where are we going to find the key?"

"She takes it to bed with her," Billy whispered.

"What?" Lauren was whispering, but it kind of sounded like she was shouting at the same time. Ma did that sometimes. Billy shrunk back. "You knew this and didn't think to tell me?"

His eyes brimmed with tears. "I thought you had another one, and that's why we were running away."

Lauren cursed again. I looked at the door, and through the blurred glass pane I could see the green of the fields we wanted to run across to escape. Turning back, I looked around the horrible, brown kitchen that always seemed to smell of soil and trash unless Lauren was cooking. I'd never hated a kitchen as much in my life. I didn't think it was possible to hate a house this much. Our plan wasn't about to be ruined. I kicked off my shoes.

"I'll get the keys," I said, placing my bag on the floor and walking over to the stairs.

"What? No! Get back here," Lauren called in her angry, loud whisper, but I kept moving.

I was halfway up the stairs in no time at all. Though my legs felt weirdly like jelly. Soft snores still floated across the hallway, giving me some confidence that the evil inside wasn't yet awake. I crept across the hallway, and a memory hit me of sneaking into my parents' kitchen to get jelly at midnight when my only friend, Lisa Middleton slept over. The thought stopped me in my tracks. That was when everything was OK. Before I ruined it all. I smiled as I remembered giggling with Lisa, wondering if we were going to get caught. That was very different to this time.

I stared at her bedroom door. It was slightly ajar which would make sneaking inside easier at least. I took a breath and snuck across the hallway, stopping when I reached the door. The snores still came. I pushed open the door. The slowest I'd ever opened a door in my life. Millimetre by millimetre the door opened. And still the snoring came.

When it was open wide enough, I stuck my head around the door frame. A dull summer light came in through the window and settled on the huge bed in the middle of the room. Ma was asleep on her side, facing the opposite way to me. For a moment, I couldn't take my eyes off her. Her fat body moved up and down in time with her snores. The blonde hair that covered her face was thick with grease. I wondered if she'd feel me watching her, like I did sometimes when Billy was standing over me at night. He only ever wanted a cuddle, but sometimes when I woke up with his face right on top of mine it made me jump.

But Ma's snores got louder as I watched, right until she snorted so loudly that she gasped and moved around in the bed. I held my breath as she turned right over. I wanted to run away but my legs were stuck to the floor. Next to the bed, a set of keys glinted on the bedside table. Right in between a half drunk glass of wine and packet of cigarettes.

"Come back down," I heard a quiet hiss from the bottom of the stairs. It was enough to wake up my stuck legs. I turned, the stairs looked so much more inviting than Ma's bedroom. But I thought about little Billy crying himself to sleep. And how Lauren took an almost daily beating - far worse than Billy and I - and I turned back to face Ma. Her eyes were closed, but she was facing me instead of the window.

This ugly, old cow will not beat me anymore.

But I needed to be quick. I tiptoed forward as slowly as I dared and prayed no floor boards would creak. I imagined her reaction if she woke up to me trying to steal her keys. Maybe I'd lie and say I was bringing her something. Breakfast in bed, or a glass of water. Except I had no water or breakfast. Maybe I could say Billy was hurt, and we needed her help. If I said it loudly enough, Billy and Lauren would hear and could pretend it was true. They'd have to take their boots off pretty quickly though.

I reached the dressing table with no creaky floorboards and reached out to the set of keys. I placed my fingers gently around the biggest key and watched Ma as I slowly lifted them up. Gently, gently, I raised them off the dressing table, wincing at the rattle they made. I didn't dare look at Ma until the keys were complete off the dressing table. But I risked a glance before I turned to walk away and looked straight into her eyes.

Her wide-open eyes.

Swanson

T hanks to the tail end of lunchtime traffic outside of the hospital, Hart was already in the kitchen when Swanson arrived at the station. It didn't surprise him to see dark bags under her eyes. Hart didn't sleep properly for at least a week after finding a dead body.

"Morning," he said in a low voice. "You look awful."

"Morning." Overcompensating as usual for her lack of sleep, she grinned widely and sang the word in a high-pitched voice. Though her smile fell when she spotted his narrowed eyes. "You have a face full of cheer as usual, I see, Swanson."

"Uh huh."

"Here." She reached into the fridge and brought out a small bottle of something. "This will make you smile."

"I'm not drinking alcohol at lunchtime, Hart." He scoffed.

Hart laughed and revealed a bottle of Fanta Lemon. Despite himself, he grinned as he took it from her; he didn't bother to mention that he'd already drank a can earlier in the day.

"There's that beautiful smile!" she mocked. "Now come on, grumps. Let's figure out our next steps."

She pulled out a chair at the kitchen table and sat down, holding a coffee in one hand and her handbag in the other. She looked up at him and cocked her head to one side.

"Your beard is going grey, you know."

He muttered something indiscernible under his breath as he pulled out a chair opposite of her and sat down.

"So, tell me what you found out, then," Hart said in a low voice. She looked around as she spoke, as if checking to make sure there was no one in the shadows.

"Who are you looking for?" he asked.

"What? No one. Go on, then. Spill."

"The victim Billy spoke about, Cara Percy, was taken from a hotel room in Derby after a night out. Police, at the time, believed her to be drugged."

"Oh, same thing he did to his current girlfriend, then."

"Yep. Only this time there was a witness. Her friend, Robin Jones, saw her being carried away. She went out drinking in Derby with Cara, and they ran into another group of friends having a drink. Two women, one man. She said the man was weird, but the women were OK. They said they were from Nottingham and had rented a hotel room in Derby for the night. After a few drinks, they all went back to the hotel room for more. One of the women, Robin didn't remember much about her, left at some point. After some drinks in the hotel room, she saw Cara passed out and stepped over to her to check she was OK. Except, Robin started to feel funny, too. As her eyes closed, she vaguely saw the man carrying Cara away. The woman left with them."

"It's strange how they just left Robin Jones there. She was a witness. She'd spent time with them and would be able to describe them. Didn't he care about getting caught?"

"It is strange, unless Cara was specifically targeted. Summer can ask Billy for more information today. Hopefully she'll get something more solid out of him."

"How's she holding up?" Hart yawned and blinked hard.

"Summer? She's fine. She's got plenty of experience with guys like Billy. I think she's fine, anyway."

"Good job, really. She's been thrown in the deep end a bit with Billy, hasn't she?"

Swanson nodded slowly as it occurred to him that he hadn't even asked Summer how she was holding up with the harrowing details of the case. But she was used to it. She'd be OK.

"So, what else did this witness say?"

"She gave a description of the man which matched Billy Bailey. And for the woman who stayed, she described her as a pretty woman in her early thirties with black hair and a tattoo on her wrist that looked like this."

He pulled out a piece of paper he'd printed off earlier that morning. It showed the image of Robin Jones's drawing of the woman's tattoo. He passed it across the table to Hart. She sipped on her coffee as she took the paper from his hand. But her eyes widened as the coffee stuck in her throat, and she spluttered all over the image. She threw it back to him as she coughed, trying to get her breath back.

"What is that?" she croaked in between wheezes.

"The tattoo. Robin Jones drew it two years ago when we interviewed her following Cara Percy's disappearance. I printed it from the original case file. Do you need some water?"

Hart took a deep breath and gave one last hacking cough. "Yes, I know it's an image of her tattoo, but what is it? What does the symbol mean? Is it a popular tattoo?"

Swanson studied the drawing once more. The brief lines inside seemed to be completely random. It wasn't a sign of anything as far as he knew.

"I have no idea. It doesn't look like anything in particular to me. I haven't seen it anywhere before. Why?" He looked back up at Hart, and she looked much paler than usual. "What's wrong with you? Do you recognise it?"

But she didn't answer. She snatched the paper back from his hand and brought it closer to her face, squinting at the drawing.

"You really need to wear your glasses." Swanson narrowed his eyes at her. She ignored him and continued to stare at the paper, twisting it left and right. "Hart?"

She looked up as though she'd forgotten he was there. "I'm not sure. Possibly. I'll be back in a minute." She threw the piece of paper back onto the table and turned on her heel towards the kitchen door.

Swanson stood, his chair scraping noisily off the kitchen tiles. "Where are you going?" he called, throwing his hands in the air.

"For a piss!" she yelled back. Without even a glance back at him, she disappeared, turning left out of the kitchen door.

The opposite direction of the toilets.

What the hell was she playing at? Swanson moved to the doorway, tripping over Hart's untucked chair in his irritation and nearly spilling the bottle of Fanta Lemon that hadn't left his hand. He stuck his head out of the kitchen doorway, just in time to see her closing the door to an interview room at the end of the corridor.

But in her haste, she'd left the door ajar.

He stepped as quietly as possible across the corridor and down towards the interview room – not an easy feat for a man with size thirteen feet. As he reached the door, he silently thanked the shoddy decorators for at least choosing soft carpet tiles. He stood on the left-hand side of the door, so she couldn't see a shadow through the glass pane. And then he leaned casually against the wall with his head cocked to one side.

"I know I said I wouldn't call you, but listen, I need a word. It's urgent. Can we meet?" There was a pause as she waited for someone to respond. "No, it can't wait…. Fine six p.m. in the car park, then."

Before he'd processed any of her conversation, the interview room door flung open and Hart was suddenly right next to him. He looked down at her, mouth partly open and one eyebrow raised. For the first time in their careers, he had no idea what to say to her. Not even a joke would come to mind.

Hart, on the other hand, cursed loudly multiple times.

"Sooo, are you going to tell me who that was?" he asked.

"No. Nobody. It's nothing. I don't want to involve them if they've got nothing to do with it, OK?"

She chewed on her bottom lip. Swanson simply continued to stare and said nothing. He didn't need to ask again. Hart couldn't keep secrets. It wasn't in her skill set. He took a slow sip of Fanta Lemon as he waited.

"OK, fine! Jesus. If you're going to keep staring me down like that, I'll tell you. You're a real arsehole sometimes. You know that? A real gem. I happen to know someone who has that tattoo, and I wondered if they'd know what it meant. That's all. It's not like they're involved."

He lowered his bottle of Fanta slowly. "Fair enough. So, who is this person? Female, I'm guessing?"

She huffed loudly. "Yes. It's a female."

"Do I know them?"

She went quiet and looked away. "They weren't involved. You don't need to know who she is."

He studied her protective expression. "I'm guessing it's an ex of yours?"

Her head snapped back around, her cheeks flushed. "What makes you say that?"

"The way you're acting. You feel strongly about her, clearly."

"I do not have any feelings for her, thank you!" She faltered. "Well, not anymore."

"For god's sake, Hart. If you trust this person, then I trust them, too. OK? You have great judgement. Just spit it out. Who has the tattoo?"

"She doesn't even have it anymore. It was lasered off years ago. But I recognise the faint pattern because it's so unusual and, well, I spent a lot of time looking at."

"Who, Hart?" Swanson cried, exasperation building up.

She sighed and looked up at him with unusually serious eyes. "It's Charlie Marsh, OK?"

It took Swanson a moment to respond. But in the second it took him to process the information, he realised Marsh was just Hart's type. She was pretty perfect for Hart, actually. Wow. How hadn't he seen that before?

"And where is Marsh now?" he asked.

"I don't know. But I'm meeting her later. And I'll be alone, Swanson. You're not questioning her."

"Of course." He nodded in agreement. "But I won't be far away, either."

Summer

Summer pulled up to the station car park just after 11:00
a.m, unsure if turning up an hour earlier than Murray
asked was weird. Or would it make a good impression?
It showed how keen she was, at least. Though she wasn't one
hundred percent sure how keen she was anymore.

However, she had nothing better to do today. Her 10:00
a.m. advocacy meeting with the hospital she'd been due at had
cancelled.

She wished she'd had time to sneak a cigarette in. Swanson
would go mad if he smelt it, though, and in all honesty she
couldn't handle the smell on her clothes these days either. It
seemed easier to quit the first time, with Joshua growing in
her belly. This time it was just her own health to think of, and
that just wasn't as motivating.

She got out of the car, let the sun warm the goose pimples
the air con had given her arms and turned towards the ugly
building as she stretched. A slight breeze rippled the thin navy
blouse she wore over black slacks. Murray stood on the steps,
staring straight at her. And she didn't look happy.

Summer stopped stretching immediately. She grabbed her
handbag from the boot of the car and made her way over
to Murray, trying to make sure she walked with a sense of

purpose. She could tell a lot about somebody from their walk. Swanson had warned her to make sure she made an amazing first impression. But just being around Murray's glare brought out immense feelings of inadequacy.

"Morning." Summer smiled at Murray, who gave a brief smile back.

"Morning, Summer. Can I have a word?"

Her heart dropped. Murray had a way about her that made Summer feel as though she'd constantly made a mistake. "Of course."

She followed Murray inside the imposing station through the rear door, and they walked in silence to Murray's office. Summer struggled to keep up with Murray's fast pace. Whatever had pissed Murray off this morning, Summer prayed it wasn't her.

They walked down the main corridor and through a door at the end which opened up into the wide office space. At the far side of the room was another door which led to Murray's office. Summer had only met Murray in the interview room before, and now that she was inside Murray's office she took full advantage of sneaking a look around to get an insight into her new boss.

She was disappointed to see that her office was quite plain, though, other than the usual desk and computer equipment, with two chairs on the opposite side. The only insight was how cold it was, and hopefully that wasn't reminiscent of Murray's management style. She gestured at Summer to take a chair on the opposite side of the desk.

"Sorry to drag you in as soon as you arrived, Summer," Murray started. Though she didn't look apologetic.

"That's OK," Summer replied.

"I just wanted to know how you are with it all. Some details of the case are quite harrowing." Murray looked away, as if a noise outside the window had caught her attention.

"Yes, they are. I'm OK, though."

Murray turned back and narrowed her eyes at Summer. "Are you absolutely sure? There's no shame in admitting it if so."

Summer tried not to get annoyed. Everyone always thought she was so sensitive and weak. Since when did introversion and kindness make someone weak? Though she was partly annoyed because, if she was honest, yes it did bother her. But who wouldn't be somewhat effected?

"The details aren't nice, but in all honesty, I've heard much worse from patients." That bit was true at least.

Murray nodded slowly. "Good. Now another reason I brought you in here, is because Charlie Marsh isn't here yet. I don't know where she is. I actually thought I saw her car in the car park, but now I can't seem to find her so Lisa Trent has gone looking. So, no interviews yet until I can get hold of them. I don't want to freak him out with somebody else if we don't have to."

"Oh." Summer hesitated. "Do you want me to do anything in particular in the meantime?"

Murray waved a hand towards her office door. "Maybe sit with the task force. They might have something for you to get involved with."

Summer left and returned to the open-plan desks, choosing to sit at one in the far corner where Murray had set up the task force. She plonked her bag on a spare desk and pulled out her phone. A text flashed up from Swanson, along with a missed call.

'Are you in the office? Are you with Trent or Marsh?'

She left her bag on the desk and wandered off to a quieter corner to call him back. He answered almost immediately.

"Hi. Trent isn't here yet. She's looking for Marsh. I'm just waiting for her."

Swanson's colourful language made her eyes widen. He didn't swear often, but he really went for it when he did. Everyone seemed mad at Marsh today. Christ! Summer would have to make sure she was never late. It clearly didn't go down well.

"Why do you need her?" she asked.

"Look, I need a chat with her about something. It's a long story, but *don't* tell her I'm after her. Can you please try to find her and keep her busy?"

Summer's brow crinkled. "Why on earth can't I tell her you want her?"

"I really can't say, Summer. It would take forever to explain. Please, just do me this favour?"

"Has she done something wrong?"

"No. I don't think so."

Summer fell silent. This was totally off and was the last thing she needed. Unease flared in her stomach.

"Is your silence a yes?" Swanson pushed.

She sighed. "Fine, but only because it's you. I don't like it at all."

"I will explain later, I promise. It's probably nothing to worry about."

And with that he hung up on her without so much as a goodbye or a thank you. Annoyance mixed with her nerves and created a nauseous swirl in her stomach. Interviewing a murderer was no problem. But lying was something she'd never been very good at. She was here to talk to people, not to lie to new colleagues who seemed perfectly nice. And anyway, Marsh wasn't even here.

Although Murray did say that her car was in the car park. Or *had* been in the car park. But Summer had no idea what car Marsh drove, so no point checking to see if it was still there. She walked back over to the task force and introduced herself to a few officers, asking if they'd seen her anywhere, but the answer was no.

The office door opened and drew her attention, and a man walked in – some officer she hadn't met yet. At the same time, Summer spotted a flash of blonde hair behind the man, and she hurried over to the door, almost barging past the poor guy. She ran down the corridor in the direction she'd spotted the blonde hair going and rounded the corner trying to catch up, colliding smack bang into Charlie Marsh.

"Watch it!" Marsh yelled.

"Oh no, I'm sorry! Are you OK?"

Marsh's haughty face broke out into a grin. "Summer? What are you doing running around here?"

"Trying to find you." *Oh no!* She knew she wasn't a good liar, so why had she agreed to this?

"What for? Is Billy ready for another interview?"

"What? Oh yes. Yes, he is. I think. Murray said so, anyway," Summer babbled, though Marsh seemed relaxed.

"OK, well, I'm just going to pick up some breakfast if that's OK. Been here since six, and my stomach's going to be shouting all the way through if I don't eat."

"Where from?" Summer asked, hoping she sounded normal.

But Marsh's grin faltered. She hesitated, then shrugged. "McDonald's, maybe. Do you want me to bring you something back?"

Summer's eyes flicked down. Marsh's left hand was shaking, so she pointed to it.

"Is your hand OK?"

"My hand?" Marsh looked down at herself.

"Yes. It's shaking."

"Oh, yes." Her grin returned, but it seemed more forced. "I gave it a pretty good bang the other night, actually. It's killing me."

"Oh, OK."

The pair looked at each other, and an awkward silence descended. Summer scanned her brain for any words that wouldn't sound suspicious.

"Murray was looking for you," she eventually blurted out.

"She was?"

A colder voice came from behind the pair. "Yes, she was."

The women turned to see Murray staring at them. Summer would have shrunk if Murray'd aimed that stare at her. Or maybe disappeared altogether.

"You can get breakfast in the kitchen, Marsh. Or later. Come on. Get Billy ready to talk, and I'll call Trent to tell her you've returned so she can do the interview."

"Sure," Marsh replied, her smile definitely false now. "I'll go get him straight away."

Summer had never loved Murray so much as in that moment. She just had to stay on her good side. She whipped out her phone to text Swanson.

'She's here. Hurry up!'

The reply came back within seconds.

'Keep her there. We're on our way.'

Swanson

S wanson checked his phone again as he hung onto the car door for dear life. Against his better judgement, he had let Hart drive them to Marsh's house in an attempt to chat with her earlier than 6:00 p.m. She'd insisted, and he thought focusing on driving would stop her flapping about Marsh.

That turned out to be a big mistake.

"Slow down, Hart. Christ."

She threw him an annoyed look. "I'm only going forty! Just because I don't drive like the car will shatter any second. They're quite strong, you know."

"Well, mine did shatter, yesterday, didn't it?" he sniped back.

They glared angrily at each other. Hart broke first, her lips curving into a smile as laughter spilled out.

"It wasn't bloody funny," Swanson snapped, but it didn't take long for his glare to ease. It wasn't a smile; it was too soon for that. But he was no longer glaring. His phone vibrated, and he snatched it up off his lap. Summer's name flashed up with a second text.

'Marsh's back. She's gone to get Billy. We're going to interview Billy, so I can't watch her.'

He repeated the text back to Hart, who huffed irritably. "OK.

Well, like I said, I'm sure there's a reasonable explanation about the tattoo, anyway."

"Then why are you driving like a lunatic? You know more than you're telling me, Rebecca Hart. Maybe our good friend, Marsh, is part of a cult, and they all have that weird-ass tattoo."

Hart shrugged. "She could easily be an *ex*-member of a cult, to be fair. Doesn't talk about her past much. She isn't in one now, though, and that's the important thing."

Swanson turned to stare at her, his eyes wide. "What do you mean she could easily be an ex-member of a cult? And how do you know she isn't in one now? Someone has been in my office messing with my chair, remember?"

Hart hit her palm on the steering wheel. "I just know. OK? Will you trust me? For once just let me do what I need to."

He turned to stare back out of the front window. "I wish you'd stop being so secretive, that's all."

She sniggered. "It's annoying, isn't it? Not sharing everything. Being all secretive. Acting all *'I work alone,'* like Batman."

"I do not do that," Swanson replied with a stubborn edge in his voice.

"You're the worst for it!" She let out a belly laugh, but Swanson didn't respond. At least her driving had slowed down, and if taking the piss out of him was what helped calm her, then so be it. She fell silent once she'd stopped laughing, and they drove along with just the radio to break up the quiet between them.

Grateful for the peace, Swanson considered the viable options. It was entirely feasible that this tattoo was more common than he'd realised. He had no tattoos, though he knew of a lot of the common ones purely thanks to arresting so many people.

But Billy didn't have any tattoos. The weirdest thing about the whole situation was Hart's reaction to seeing it. Almost like it confirmed something for her, as though she'd already had suspicions something was wrong with Marsh. But was it really possible that Marsh had known who Billy Bailey was the second he walked into the police station?

"Do you think Marsh knows Billy Bailey? I mean, this woman at the scene didn't do anything. She just happened to be staying with him and then left *with* him," he thought aloud to Hart.

"No. He would have said in the interviews. Wouldn't he?" Hart answered.

"Unless they were working together."

"Swanson! Your mind always goes to the absolute worst possible place in every situation. This is *Marsh*. We've known her for a couple of years. She isn't in partnership with possibly the most heinous serial killer Derby has ever seen."

"The country, you mean," Swanson muttered.

"Well, the country doesn't know that yet, do they? Because once they do, the bloody media will be everywhere."

"We don't know that either, to be fair. Who knows what's actually happened."

"He's told us where all the bodies are so far. Do you still think he didn't do it?" Hart asked as she pulled into the station car park.

Swanson tugged at his beard. "I don't know. He clearly helped bury the bodies at the very least. There's just something... *off* about the whole thing. There's something not right about it all."

"Her car is there now." Hart motioned with one hand as she reversed into a bay near the exit, making no effort to make sure it was straight.

"Good, let's go find her then." Swanson practically ran out of the car.

"*I* will talk to her, Swanson. *You* need to let go and find somewhere to sit for a while. No arguments!" she added with a raised hand as he opened his mouth to interject.

"Fine," he muttered as they walked towards the station.

Inside, there was no one around in the corridors. They were all squirrelled away in the office on the Billy Bailey task force, which was growing bigger by the day.

"Go wait in your office. I'll find Marsh," Hart commanded.

"Are you looking for me?" a voice called from down the corridor behind them. Marsh's head poked out from Swanson's own office door.

"OK. Go wait somewhere else," Hart muttered under her breath and headed towards Marsh.

Swanson glared at Marsh. *Why the hell was she in his office?* She smiled sweetly back at him. He imagined her smashing his car windscreen. Would Marsh really do that? He felt a sudden flare of concern and made a move to follow Hart. But she put her hand out, still staring at Marsh.

"Go, Swanson," she said in no uncertain terms.

He ignored his screaming instincts and stepped back, leaving Hart to go in and face Marsh alone.

Marsh

Charlie Marsh turned back into Swanson's office as Hart walked towards her. She put one hand to her chest to calm her heart and took a deep breath. How could she be stupid enough to let them catch her inside Swanson's office? A multitude of different excuses ran through her mind, but this was Rebecca Hart. And she'd never been good at lying to people she loved.

The walls of Swanson's small space were closing in, causing beads of sweat to gather on her forehead. Only God knew how he could work in this room. Aside from the tight space, the desk was a mess, too. It was a struggle to find anything. She plastered on a fake smile and leaned against the desk. She kept her eyes down on the floor, trying to look casual – bored, even.

But it was pretty clear the pair knew something from the look Hart had given her. She looked so serious, and not in an angry way anymore. Hart had been angry at her for months. But she'd looked at her with sadness in her eyes. Or fear. Maybe Billy had finally cracked and told them about her.

It didn't matter what Hart knew. Something had made her suspicious of Marsh, and only the truth might save her now. She imagined the look on Hart's face as she told her what really happened. Hart already hated her, but that might have died down in time. Knowing the truth would cause her to hate her forever. The thought gripped Marsh's heart like a vice, causing an ache worse than when they'd broken up.

She heard Hart's footsteps coming down the corridor; the sharp thud of her heels made sure everyone always knew when Hart was on her way. She'd be the new Murray one day. Marsh was sure of it. She had that way about her. Cool, calm and brutal. Her eyes were drawn to a file on Swanson's desk.

Damn!

She hadn't put Billy's file away. How could she have been so stupid? It was partly Swanson's fault she'd seen the file. He'd left it easily accessible inside the top drawer of his desk. Too simple for anyone to find, really. She'd always thought he was so meticulously careful about everything. But then again, his desk was a mess. And he wouldn't have expected a fellow officer to go snooping.

She quickly leaned over and wiped it off the desk. It fell on the floor at the side with a quiet thud. She cursed her own stupidity for coming into his office in the middle of the day. Summer had said they'd be out for a while. Was she in on whatever they knew?

She should have left the file well alone. All the key information was in the system, anyway. Other than Swanson's personal suspicions and notes. They were only in his own paper file, and now she knew what he thought. His unjustified conviction that Billy was not the killer. Poor Billy was just some sort of puppet, or maybe a crazy person.

Swanson was right about both.

Hart's footsteps reached the door, and she stormed in and slammed the door behind her. She paused, took a deep breath, and then turned to Marsh. OK, maybe she wasn't sad. She was mad. Definitely mad.

"Marsh. What the hell is going on? Why are you in Swanson's office looking as guilty as when I walked in on you and Trent?"

So, it was searching Swanson's office that had alerted suspicion, then. Hart's voice was calmer than expected. It didn't match the fiery expression on her face at all.

"I was looking for you," Marsh lied in a last-ditch effort, her eyes wide and as trusting as she could make them. She knew she was a good liar. Excellent, in fact. Just not against Hart. But if she could get Hart to believe her, then it wouldn't matter about anyone else.

Hart was also an excellent lie detector, and her face hardened further.

"Cut the bullshit. I know when you're lying," she snapped, her tone angrier.

Marsh sighed and looked down. "I was just looking for Billy's file. I thought Swanson would have notes in it that he didn't want to share yet, and it would have been helpful in the interview."

"Wrong again," Hart snapped. She crossed her arms, eyes narrowed.

The knot in Marsh's stomach tugged and turned and made her feel sick. Her legs gave way, and she found herself sitting in Swanson's chair. She would have to admit the truth to the one woman she really loved, and the ugliness of it all was almost too much to bear.

Summer

S ummer leaned against the counter in the kitchen, relieved that her stint in lying to Marsh was over. And hopefully Marsh would never know of her involvement. Lying always made things worse. Her mum had instilled that within her from a very young age. As much as she loved her dad, he was terrible for lying. He'd lie about what he ate for breakfast for no reason. She smiled. She'd give anything to hear one more daft lie from him.

She fingered the beautiful rose gold watch strapped to her wrist. It was a gift from her younger brother last Christmas. Her eyes were drawn to the clock face. It was close to 2:00 p.m. Almost time to pick up Joshua from school, so she'd have to get going soon.

Heavy thuds in the corridor made her look up at the doorway. Swanson appeared seconds later, his forehead creased and jaw clenched. An urge to reach out to him pulled at her, but she kept it at bay. He clearly wasn't in the mood for a hug. He didn't even look up.

"Hi," she said tentatively.

His head shot up, and he looked at her as if surprised to see her there. But his forehead softened, and he gave her a small smile.

"Hi," he replied. He didn't move towards her, and stood awkwardly at the other side of the kitchen. Summer tried to ignore the tension between them, which seemed to get worse every time they met at work.

"Are you going to tell me what's going on with Marsh?" she asked.

His forehead creased again. "I don't know what's going on with Marsh. Hart's talking to her now. I'm sure it's nothing."

"It didn't seem like nothing." Summer looked away. It was obvious he was lying, but why? Why would he lie to her?

"Well, it's *probably* nothing. I'm really not sure. Hart wouldn't tell me the full story." He leaned against the counter with his arms crossed.

"It's OK if you can't tell me. Have you found out anything you *can* tell me?"

"About what?"

"About Billy Bailey, what else?"

"Nothing. No. There's nothing else." He busied himself with making a glass of water, unable to look her in the eye. "I spoke to Marcie."

"How is she?" Summer raised her voice over the noise of the running tap.

"She was OK, considering what happened to her. Still in hospital, but she was happy to talk. Well, she was until I asked her about the Cara Percy case." He turned off the tap and drank the pint of water in a few gulps.

"What about the Cara Percy case?"

"I looked up the case this morning and spoke to a friend who was out with Cara that night. She saw Cara being taken away by a man matching Billy's description."

"That adds up, then."

"Yes, but there were two women with him. One left, and one stayed."

"That night? So, there was Cara, her friend, and two other women with Billy. If we assume the man was Billy. So, he was out with four women that night and only murdered one."

"It looks that way."

"Do you think Marcie knew what was going on?"

"I have no idea. But this woman had a tattoo on her left wrist, and Marcie doesn't have one. I checked." Swanson pulled open the dishwasher to place his empty glass on the top shelf.

Summer considered what he was saying. She thought about James Evans. Unsure whether to mention him. Was it relevant? Swanson seemed so antsy.

"Do we know who the young boy they found at Bell Woods is yet?"

"Not yet."

"I know a boy who went missing nearby when we were about sixteen. He was a friend of mine. I was wondering if it might be him."

"What was his name?"

"James Evans."

Swanson brought one hand up to his beard. "James? That rings a bell from somewhere."

"It does?" Summer stood up straight, her heart pounding as thoughts of the happy, fun-loving boy she knew ran through her mind.

"I can't think where—" He snapped his fingers. "Robin Jones. She said the man that night introduced himself as James. That might mean nothing, though. I mean, how long ago did he go missing?"

"About fifteen years ago. He didn't have a great home life.

We all thought he'd run away, and so did the police."

"Well, I'll look into it. Hopefully, you're right and he ran away."

"Thanks. Do you want me to ask Billy about this tattoo?"

Swanson froze, midway through closing the dishwasher door. "Not yet. I just need to find out about something. I've probably been in here for over five minutes now, right?"

"Er, probably." Summer looked at her watch again. "Yes, just about five minutes."

"OK. I need to go."

Summer shrugged. It was infuriating getting anywhere with Swanson sometimes, but now they were supposedly on the same team it was even harder. He stopped at the kitchen door and turned to her.

"Look, Summer. It's a strange job. I will tell you everything I know as soon as I know what's actually happening, OK?"

She nodded. He always seemed to read her mind. It was funny really, considering she was the psychology expert. There was a long-running inside joke that everyone assumes a psychologist can read your thoughts and predict your movements. Yet when it came to Swanson, she felt useless.

The Runaway - 19 Years Before

Ma gave no reaction to the keys in my hand. I'd never felt so happy in my entire life as I did when her eyes drifted shut. How could she not hear my heart beating? It felt like it was going to break free and I'd die right there in front of her, hands still gripping the keys. But her eyes closed completely, and the snoring began again. I didn't dare breathe and backed away on my tiptoes, watching her the whole time.

It wasn't until the door dug into my back that I was brave enough to turn around. My legs had gone from being stuck to the floor to being full of extra energy and I had to try extra hard not to run or make any noise. When I reached the top of the stairs, Lauren and Ben were looking up at me with wide eyes and worried smiles.

"Did you get them?" Lauren whispered.

I nodded, still not daring to make a noise. I crept down the stairs, smiling so much my mouth hurt, and handed Lauren the keys. She unlocked the door as I put on my shoes, and within minutes we were free. I waited until we were outside to laugh, and we ran as fast as we could down the farm's long driveway. Well, I'd found out it wasn't really a farm. It used to be before Ma's husband died, but now it just had some buildings with chickens and ducks and boring things.

But it didn't matter now, we were free.

We ran into the field opposite the driveway and kept running until Billy slowed down and struggled to keep up. I didn't want to admit it because Lauren was fine, but my chest was on fire by then, anyway. So I was secretly glad when he asked us to slow down. Billy and I panted like dogs in the morning sunshine while Lauren rolled her pretty eyes.

"Come on slow pokes," she moaned. "Let's go find us a new home! Where shall we go?"

"Let's sleep in a tent!" Billy shouted.

"Where are we going to get a tent from, eh? Or sleeping bags?" Lauren replied.

Billy's face fell. He was so stupid sometimes but he was smaller than us. I think Lauren forgot she was four years older than him.

"Well, we can't go to the police because they'll take us back to her," I said.

"Obviously," Lauren replied, flicking back her long hair. Her hair always looked so much better than mine, even though neither of us were allowed shampoo. "Do either of you have any family left? Like nice ones, obviously."

"I have a brother," Billy announced proudly.

"A brother?" I asked, wondering why they weren't together.

"Yes." He nodded his head defiantly. "I had a brother when I was very little but he moved out, and then my step dad came to live with us. But he kept being mean, so I set fire to him and they took me away."

Years ago, I'd heard my mum use the expression 'I thought my eyeballs were going to pop out of my head'. It wasn't until that moment that I truly understood what she meant. I turned to Lauren. Her mouth hung open just like mine did.

"You set fire to him?" she asked.

It surprised me she could speak, my words were all lost in my throat somewhere. Billy nodded. He showed no sign of understanding that it wasn't normal to set your step dad on fire.

"Yes. He was OK, though. He didn't die or anything. Anyway, he doesn't like me very much and I'm not allowed to do it ever again. But my big brother was nicer. I bet he'd give us a tent!"

"Hmm." Lauren turned away, shielding her eyes from the sun with one hand as she looked across the field. "Where does he live?"

"Erm," Billy pointed across the field. "That way, I think."

"No, Billy. Like what town does he live in?"

"Spondon. It's in Derby." He grinned wider than I'd ever seen him grin.

"OK. We need to sneak on a train to Derby," Lauren replied and walked off.

Billy and I followed her across the soft grass. It was hard to keep up; she had longer legs than us and walked so quickly. We arrived at another stile, and I helped push Billy over the top before I climbed over myself. When I reached the other side, Lauren was a few hundred yards ahead of us. Talking to a man. I froze and pulled Billy close to me. The man was pretty old, at least forty years old. He was tanned and bald with huge hands. Lauren flicked her hair and laughed as he spoke. She had a sweet laugh. And the man seemed to like it. She turned and waved us over.

"This is Lee," she said as we reached them. She smiled proudly. I still held on tightly to Billy's hand. "He's going to take us to the train station."

"OK," I replied without smiling. I didn't like the look of Lee, though he smiled at Billy and I too.

"Don't worry." He reached out with one hand and rested it on my shoulder.

I fought an urge to shrug it off.

"I don't bite. I'll take you where you want to go," he said.

Lauren and Lee led the way as Billy and I trailed behind. Billy let go of my hand and grinned up at me. I seemed to be the only one of us who didn't immediately like Lee. It didn't take long to reach the edge of the field, where Lee walked over to a truck parked at the side of the road.

"Here we go, guys," he called out as he opened the enormous door. He pulled back the driver's seat and Billy and I climbed in the back, which was tight for such a big truck. Lauren moved to the other side to get in the front seat.

"You too," Billy pointed to the back seat. "It's safer in there."

Lauren shrugged and climbed in the back with us too, Billy squished into the middle of us and held both our hands.

"Let's go!" Cried Lee as he jumped into the front seat.

He pulled off and drove to the edge of the dirt road he'd parked the truck on. He indicated right to reach the main road and spent some time checking both directions. Too long for saying it was so early and absolutely nobody was on the road. His phone beeped, and he looked down to check it. That seemed to be what he was really waiting for. Because once he'd read that, he sped away.

In the wrong direction.

"Hey, Lee! We need to go that way," called out Lauren. "The train station is that way!"

"Just taking a slight detour, little lady."

He sped up and Billy squeezed my hand tighter. I looked at

Lauren, she'd paled and was no longer smiling.

"Where's the detour too, Lee?" she asked, her voice suddenly much mousier.

"You'll see," he replied. His smile was gone too., replaced with a hard look. And as he hurtled down the road, we knew there was only one thing at the end.

Ma's farm.

Marsh

Marsh sucked her cheek in as she tried to hold back tears. Hart's footsteps edged closer, passing the small gap between them, but she didn't bother to look up. What was the point? It would only be hatred in Hart's eyes from the second she knew the truth, and the pain of Hart hating her on top of everything else was almost too much to bear. But to her surprise, she felt a gentle hand on her shoulder.

"Charlie?"

Hart's tone was soft with no trace of the anger that had laced it earlier. Marsh raised her head in surprise. She hadn't heard Hart say her first name in at least three months. She racked her brain to remember. The last time was probably when they shared a bed together for the final time. Right before Hart thought she walked in on Marsh with another woman - Lisa Trent. She placed her own hand over Hart's.

"Tell me what's really happening. I trust you. I just want to help, and to do that I need to know what's going on with you," Hart continued.

"I can't." Marsh choked on the words, the lump in her throat now the size of an orange. It made it difficult to breathe, never mind speak.

"You can." Hart squeezed the hand resting on Marsh's shoulder and brought it down to place it on her knee. "You can tell me anything, remember?"

Marsh focused on Hart's fingers, wrapped around her own. She traced Hart's thumb with her own forefinger, but pulled her hand away roughly. "That was before I messed things up between us."

"Yes, before you cheated. But that doesn't matter anymore. This is serious, and I can still help you if you open up to me." She put one hand on her hip.

Marsh sighed. Her eyes closed as she tried to think of the right words to tell Hart. The enormity of what she was about to say weighed heavily on her heart.

"I didn't cheat on you, Rebecca." Hart's first name felt strange to say out loud now. As if it was a naughty word she wasn't allowed to say. "But as hard as it was, you believing that I'd cheated was better than telling you the truth."

Hart sat back. "You let me think you'd cheated on me with Trent? What were you doing with her, then?"

"She knew something was off with me and cornered me. She's so intense, but I convinced her I had family issues. Which is actually true, but she doesn't know the full truth and I didn't want to admit to you that she'd grown suspicious of me hiding something. It's a very, very long story."

"Long story? That's fine. I've got all day." Hart stomped to the other side of the desk and pulled round a second chair. She plonked it directly in front of Marsh and sat down, her legs and arms both stubbornly crossed. "Actually, it would be hilarious to see Swanson's face if this did take all day. He'd be raging."

Despite herself, Marsh chuckled softly. "What does he

know?"

"He knows you have a tattoo similar to one a woman at a previous crime scene had. That's all he knows. Hell, that's all I know."

"Does he know about us?" Marsh asked nervously. It was no secret that both of them liked women, but personal relationships weren't exactly encouraged between officers. Murray would certainly have had a word to say about it. The last thing she wanted was for Hart to get into trouble.

"Yes. He won't say anything about that, though. He doesn't care too much about personal goings-on and he's shagging the new bird anyway, so he can't say anything."

Marsh laughed again, harder this time. It was impossible not to around Hart. "You're vulgar."

"I know I am. Being vulgar and carefree is part of my charm. Now tell me, come on. Let me help. Were you with Billy the night he took Cara Percy?"

Marsh shook her head vehemently. "No, no. Of course not. Not when she was taken, anyway."

"That tattoo you had lasered off, was it this?" Hart brought out a sheet of paper with a drawing on it. A drawing that made Marsh feel sick to her stomach. She tried to speak, but she lost the words in her throat, so she nodded her head instead.

"The woman who was with Billy had this. I need to know what it means, so I can try to find out who the other woman is. Billy won't talk about her."

"This tattoo is something someone made up when I was a kid," Marsh muttered. "It means nothing in particular."

"OK. So, who else has one? You know who we're looking for, don't you?"

"When I was a kid—" Marsh faltered. This would be the first

time telling anybody the full truth about her childhood. She looked again at Hart, whose face was so serious. If she was going to be forced to tell anyone, at least it was Hart.

She started again.

"You already know my parents died when I was a kid, and they sent me to foster care. I've never told you much more than that because the rest is too hard to talk about. I've spent my life trying to forget it. There was another girl there, and a boy. The foster carer was in it for the money. The system is much different these days, luckily, but that's thanks in part to evil witches like her coming to light and extra safeguarding being put in place. Although no one ever caught her for what she did." Marsh shuddered at the memory of arriving to meet Ma for the first time. The smell of apple pie was still sickening. "The little boy was Billy, and the girl was named Lauren. We would do everything around the house. Cooking, cleaning, washing. She'd beat the hell out of all three of us otherwise."

Hart gasped. "Jesus, Charlie. I'm so sorry you had to go through that."

"That was just the beginning. Then we met Lee. A huge guy who did worse things than beat us. He was a tattooist. He tattooed both us girls and told us we were his forever now. He'd make Billy do things to us whilst he watched, and then he'd take a turn, too."

"What a sick prick," Hart spat. She uncrossed her arms and legs, and one hand flew to her stomach as if she was nauseous. Marsh understood that. It made her feel nauseous thinking about it, too. Her voice cracked as she continued.

"It was our fault-"

"No!" Hart snapped. "You don't use those words. It is never the child's fault. You know this."

"I mean, the fact that Lee entered our lives, that was our fault. We tried running away one morning and ran straight into him. He agreed to take us to the train station so we jumped into the car with him. He took us straight back to that woman. Turned out he lived down the road. He knew Ma and he knew about us and she'd mentioned she was looking after *disturbed* children and to make sure he took us back to her if he ever saw us."

"That manipulative bitch," Hart spat.

"I was *so* terrified all the time, but eventually Lauren snapped. She hid a knife under her pillow. Lee climbed on top of her one night… and she pulled it out and stabbed Lee over and over and over while Billy and I watched on." Marsh's voice broke completely. The words were just too hard to say, memories too painful. Hart had found a tissue from somewhere and shoved it into her hand.

"Do you need a break?" Hart asked in a soft voice.

Marsh shook her head and swallowed down tears. The darkness of the past was clawing at her skin and revealing the ugly scars underneath for Hart to see. But she may as well get the whole sorry story out now. Alone, and with Hart, in a small, dark room was better than the glaring lights of the interview room with Murray and god knows who else.

"At that point, our foster mum had heard Lee yelling and came running upstairs. She saw Lee covered in blood and ran over to him, pulling him off Lauren. Lauren just lay there on the bed, covered in his blood. She was silent and staring at the ceiling. It was awful, yet she had a huge grin on her face. Our foster mum went mad and started hitting Lauren over and over. Lauren didn't even seem to notice the whacks at first, she was too lost in what she had done to Lee. But Ma hit her across the face and Lauren came alive again. She stabbed our foster mum, too. She fell on the floor. I can still see her gagging for her last breaths, reaching out to me for help. But I didn't move, and neither did Billy. We let her die. We watched her die and hoped she wouldn't wake up."

"That's understandable, Charlie. You were children, terrified and abused by this very woman."

"I know. I didn't even feel guilty. You'd think I would, right? Maybe normal people would. But I felt nothing but relief. I was just as complicit in that murder as Lauren. I wanted that bitch dead, and I let her die. She showered to wash the blood off. We packed some clothes, food and money - and we legged it. We laughed the whole time. We were euphoric to be getting away from them. I don't know what happened to the bodies. Nobody came looking for us. No one seemed to care much about finding us. Lee took lots of pictures, though. I imagine, knowing what I know now, that police found the pictures of us and the government covered the whole thing up to protect the reputation of the care industry. That's just how it was back then."

Hart leaned forward and reached out again, squeezing Marsh's hand gently. "What happened to your sister? Did Billy hurt her?"

Marsh snorted. "Billy would never generally hurt anyone. He doesn't really show emotion. He never learned how to with his god-awful parents. You see, my parents were amazing. I knew what love was before I went into foster care. But Billy never had that other than with me and our sister. He went into foster care because his parents beat the crap out of him from day one. Although he did set his step dad on fire once, but only because he felt he had no other choice. *We're* the only people he loves. And the only ones who have ever loved him. He doesn't even get mad, generally speaking. You could beat him to an inch of his life, and he's unlikely to even hit back. I've seen that happen to him more than once. The reason Billy is admitting to these murderers is that he's protecting our sister. Because once she murdered our foster parents, she couldn't stop killing."

She watched Hart's face pale rapidly. "Your sister is the murderer? Lauren?"

Marsh shook her head and gave Hart a sad smile. "Her name isn't Lauren anymore. It's Marcie. Marcie Livingstone."

Swanson

Swanson stood in the station car park and checked his phone for the millionth time. He was waiting for a sign from Hart on where this tattoo might have come from, but they'd been in his office almost half an hour and there was still nothing. His fists clenched. The urge to smoke a cigarette was overwhelming, but Summer would kill him if she smelt it. Or even worse, she'd use his poor decision to smoke again herself. And he would not be responsible for that.

Maybe he should barge into his office and talk to Marsh, too. It was his office, after all. What was she even doing in there? He could pretend he'd forgotten something. His case file was in there. He could grab that. Or maybe he needed a notepad. Or anything really. They'd been in there far too long. He had to make sure Hart was OK somehow.

He turned towards the station door, his decision made. He would barge into his own office and check if they were OK. He would ask if they needed anything. That was all. But as he reached for the door handle, the door flew open and Summer was suddenly in front of him.

She stood in the doorway, mouth half open as if surprised to see him. He'd felt the same way earlier in the kitchen. Suddenly, they were in each other's pockets and always running into each other when they were trying to deal with their own thoughts. She hid her surprise with a quick smile.

"Fancy seeing you here," she quipped as she exited the doorway and let the door close behind her.

"Who'd have thought it, eh?" He smiled awkwardly and took a step back.

She cocked her head. "Why are you lurking outside, though? I thought you needed to be somewhere?"

He shrugged. "I'm not welcome yet, apparently. I was getting some fresh air whilst thinking about this Billy case. Did you get the chance to speak to him today before Hart collared Marsh?"

She shook her head. "No. Have you not spoken to Hart yet?"

As he was about to answer, his phone vibrated in his hand and he almost whooped in his anticipation. He looked down to see a message from Hart. He looked back at Summer.

Fuck it.

There was only one way to find out if this working together was going to be OK.

"Fancy a field trip, Summer?" he asked. A coy smile lined his face.

She looked around as if wondering if it was her he meant to ask. "Er, OK. What about Murray, though?"

"I'll text her. She'll be fine. It's about Billy's case. Come on."

Swanson turned and rushed over to the far corner of the car park, where he meticulously parked his newly repaired Audi away from all other cars and human beings. He heard Summer's footsteps struggling to keep up behind him, and sent Murray a brief text saying he had a safe lead on Billy's case and was taking Summer with him for experience whilst Marsh was AWOL.

"Where is this field trip going?" Summer called.

"The hospital," he yelled back across the car park.

He had strapped in and was ready to pull off by the time Summer reached his car.

"Come on," he said as she opened the door. "Gotta run sometimes, Summer."

"Run? Jesus, I haven't run anywhere since year six PE."

"Why specifically year six PE? There's definitely a story there."

She sighed as she strapped in her seatbelt. "Do you remember those poppers? They were joggers that had popping buttons all the way down the outside of each leg?"

Both of Swanson's eyebrows raised. "Yes?" he said in a slow, deliberate tone.

"Well, let's just say I was running in a pair doing cross country, and I ended up having quite an embarrassing time of it."

"As in…"

Summer laughed. "You want to hear me say it? Someone pulled both sides completely open, and my pants were on show to pretty much the entire school. So, I refused to go to PE for the rest of year six, and I certainly wasn't interested by the time I got to secondary school. I had other things to worry about."

Swanson laughed heartily. "Well, you need to make sure you wear proper trousers in this job, because you need to keep going whether or not someone pulls them down."

She smiled, and the awkwardness of earlier on seemed to have dissipated. "I'll remember that. Who are we going to see at the hospital, then?"

"Little miss victim might not be a victim, after all."

Summer stared at him. "Marcie?"

He nodded as he gripped the steering wheel for a rough right turn. This school time traffic really needed to go away.

"Really? Marcie? Well, she got her head caved in, so she was a victim of something."

"Good point. Look, there's been a bit of a development, and Hart and I are trying to piece some things together. I might need you to speak to Billy about them later."

"You want me to speak to him alone?"

"No," Swanson replied quickly., imagining Murray's face at the suggestion "That can't happen."

Summer huffed. "I am capable, you know."

"Yes, I know that. But Murray wouldn't allow it yet. Things like that don't go down well in court. It all has to be above board. I can sit in with you, if you like."

Summer didn't answer. He glanced at her, silently begging her to agree. Eventually, she shrugged and nodded.

"OK. At least you know the background well," she said.

"Exactly."

"What's this development, then?"

"Well, I don't have the full story, which is why I didn't want to tell you anything yet. But it's from the woman with the strange tattoo on her wrist."

"What did it look like?" Summer sounded intrigued.

"A random pattern I'd never seen before. I showed it to Hart, she went white, and eventually after some persuasion admitted that DI Marsh had that pattern lasered off on her wrist."

"Marsh?" Summer gave him a confused glance. "What the hell does she have to do with it? Does she understand the pattern or something?"

"That's what Hart went to find out while I waited outside.

That's why I was so on edge. They were taking ages. It's a simple question. I don't get what took so long."

"I don't get what Marsh has to do with anything. She doesn't know Billy, surely?"

"Neither do I, fully, but this is a pretty unique tattoo, and she's involved somehow. All I know now is Hart texted me and told me to check on Marcie and possibly bring her in for questioning if the doctor will allow it. Hart now thinks Marcie is the *murderer* of the bodies we found in the woods."

Summer's mouth fell open. "I don't believe all this. She's the one in the hospital with a caved-in face."

"Yup. It's pretty messed up. Like I said, I don't have the full story yet."

Summer sat back in her chair. "Is this what working for the police is like all the time?"

Swanson grinned, tempted to say yes after how crazy the last year had been. But this was going pretty well so far; no need to scare her off just yet. "No. This is a pretty unusual case. But Murray seems to like Hart and I to be involved in the stranger ones. Maybe she thinks we have a penchant for them."

But a thought suddenly hit Swanson. The tattoo on the arm. The notes from the case file. He fiddled with the centre console of the car, bringing up the number of Robin Jones. It rang out for a few seconds with no answer until the voicemail picked it up.

"Hi, Robin. It's Detective Inspector Alex Swanson again. I'm on my way to your house if you can please call me back to let me know if you're there. Thank you."

"I thought we were going to the hospital?" asked Summer.

"We are. I just said that because she will—" The noise of

Robin Jones calling him back cut him off. He grinned at Summer and answered the call.

"Hi, Robin. Thanks for calling me back."

"I'm not in right now, so you can't come over."

"Oh, OK. Well, it was just a quick question if you have a spare second now?"

"Yes, yes. Ok."

"When you saw Cara being taken away, were you looking straight at them?"

"Yes, of course. I said that before. The mirror was right in front of me, and I saw them all leave through it."

"A mirror?"

"Yes, I saw them leave through the mirror."

"OK. That's all I wanted to know. Thank you, Robin."

"Are you going to explain what that was about?" Summer asked.

"I was looking at Marcie's left wrist for a tattoo. I didn't check her right because I wasn't thinking straight. If Robin saw them in a mirror, she was probably confused. Drugged and falling asleep, trying to check on her friend. Easily done."

"How did you know she was going to call back so quickly?"

"I didn't. I just guessed. Her partner has a disliking to us apparently."

Summer didn't speak again until they reached the hospital, and neither did he. Lost in his thoughts about sweet Marcie and how she could possibly be a killer. Never mind a serial killer. As he parked up, though, Summer gave him a strange look.

"I'm not buying it. Who the hell attacked Marcie if she is the killer?"

"I'm assuming it was still Billy, or possibly a survivor?"

"A survivor would come forward, though, surely. *If* it is true, which is a big if. Maybe Billy found out about the murders and attacked her?"

Summer slammed the car door behind her far too harshly. Swanson winced, but she laughed at him.

"The car won't break from me closing the door, Swanson! Honestly."

"Hey, I only just got her back! And no, they wouldn't necessarily come forward. Not if they had a record, or some other reason to hide themselves. Or even if it was a man she tried to attack. Let's face it, it's likely a man would be done for assault at least, regardless of whether or not she tried to kill him. You know what the media can be like," Swanson replied as they entered the hospital.

Once again, he breathed through his mouth to keep the smell of the hospital at bay. They marched through the winding corridors, Summer hot on his heels this time. It felt strange to have her close by, but he had to admit it was kind of nice. They reached Marcie's ward in minutes, and Swanson pushed the buzzer for a nurse to allow them inside. An older lady with deep wrinkles opened the door. Her name tag said *Irene*.

"Hello. Visiting hours aren't for another two hours, I'm afraid, guys," she said, though she gave them a friendly smile. At least she was nicer than that last nurse.

Swanson flashed his ID and his own smile. "We are looking for Marcie, please. We need an urgent word with her about her case."

"Marcie?" Irene's smile dropped, replaced by a worried look. "Oh dear. I'm afraid Marcie's gone, love."

A shot of fear stabbed Swanson's stomach. "Marcie's gone? Gone where? She can't have gone too far with that bandage

174

around her head."

"We don't know, dear. She left early this morning whilst we were in a handover meeting. She was there one minute, and gone the next."

"You allowed her to just leave?" Summer asked, forgetting this wasn't like her usual hospitals.

"We aren't a prison." Irene glowered at Summer, suddenly defensive. "Patients may come and go as they please, though we will strongly discourage it where necessary. We did not chain her to her bed, but in any case, she snuck out herself. There was only one of us on the ward whilst we had the meeting – a trainee nurse. She told that nurse she wanted a smoke and would be back in a few minutes."

Swanson brought Irene's attention back to him. "It's imperative that we find her as soon as possible, please, if you can help us with any further information?"

Irene looked Swanson up and down. "She was close to one of the younger nurses. Let me get her, and you can have a chat. Come in."

The pair stepped inside and sat down in two plastic chairs near the entrance. A few seconds later, the younger nurse walked over to them. She'd scraped her dirty blonde hair back into an unyielding bun, and large bags sat under her pretty, brown eyes.

"Hello, officers." She smiled despite her obvious tiredness. "I'm Bessie."

Swanson stood. Summer followed suit. "Hi, Bessie. I understand you might know a little more about Marcie?"

She nodded. "Yes. I'm quite worried about her, actually. I wasn't here when she disappeared, but she always seemed quite nervous. Like she was waiting for someone she didn't want to see come in. She was always looking at the door. Not surprising after what happened to her."

"No." Swanson agreed. "Well, it's very urgent that we talk to her and make sure she's OK. Did she mention where she might go?"

"She said she was desperate to go home, but I don't know where her home is specifically."

"OK. Did she say anything else or mention the name of the man she was looking out for?" Swanson asked.

"Well, she didn't name anyone." Bessie hesitated, unsure how to explain. "But the person she was scared of wasn't a man. It was a woman. She kept saying 'she.'"

"Did she give you a description of this woman?"

"A short one. She asked me to watch out for a woman in her thirties with thick blonde hair. She was real scared of her."

Swanson's stomach dropped. Marcie, the supposed murderer, was scared of DI Marsh. And Hart was all alone with her, lapping up every word she said.

Marsh

The look in Hart's eye as she stared at Marsh's stomach was one of nauseating sympathy. Marsh's cheeks flamed. When they dated, she'd refused to get fully naked in front of Hart. And the look in her eyes right now was the reason why. Then there were the questions that would have inevitably come.

So, like all of her other relationships, they hadn't lasted longer than a few months. And Hart would definitely be dating someone else by now. She'd had that look about her for a couple of weeks. Hopefully, it was someone who actually deserved her this time.

But now she had little choice but to bear the marks on her stomach, and hope they would be evidence enough for Hart to believe her story. Marsh didn't look down. She rarely did. The thought of seeing the circular cigarette marks and line after line of small slash marks made her want to die.

"So, this was what that foster woman did to you?" Hart asked in a voice much smaller than usual.

Marsh pulled down her shirt. "Part of it, yes. But she did worse to Marcie. She was older than Billy and me. I was eleven when I moved there. Billy was about eight. Marcie was thirteen."

"Sick bastards," Hart spat. Her hand tremoured.

"All these years, Billy and I have protected Marcie. Billy does anything she asks. I've tried to stop her. But it was never enough. She's broken inside. There is only one way to fix her."

Hart cleared her throat and shifted in the chair. It was hard to tell if she was hiding tears. Hart was always hard to read. But her eyes were certainly redder than usual.

"What happened after you ran away from the home?" she asked.

"Well, we were older by then. Four years had passed whilst we suffered at that woman's hands. Marcie looked old enough to be our big sister. I looked much older, too. Billy just followed us around. He didn't speak much. Never has done. Marcie found us a place to stay eventually, with a bunch of hippies."

"Did they look after you?"

Marsh hesitated. "Yes, as long as we looked after them. But they were gentle, and we didn't mind. It was nice after what we'd been through. And they left Billy alone."

"OK." Hart cleared her throat and shifted again, but this time her face hardened. "So, these women that someone has murdered, what happened to them?"

"When we were with those hippies, after a couple of years of moving around with them, they met some other girls. Marcie didn't like it. She got jealous and stabbed two of them in a house in Ilkeston. Stabbed them in their sleep and stole their things. The guys went mad, panicked and made us bury the bodies in the woods. But we had to run away again. This time she was old enough to get a job, cash in hand at a restaurant. We got our own place through the restaurant owner. He had a small flat above the eatery and took pity on us." Marsh lost her words as she remembered the grim walls of the dark flat, and the excitement they shared at moving into their first proper home.

"Charlie? Go on," Hart urged.

"Marcie was OK for a while. I thought she was OK, anyway. I started washing dishes in the restaurant and earning money, too. But one night she brought a girl up to the flat. A stunning girl, who spoke posh. She was nervous and kinda quiet, but Marcie had promised her a drink and a party. We were all sitting there – me and Billy wondering what was going on. Marcie got a knife, went mad and killed the girl. It shocked Billy and me. This time, though, Marcie said she knew how to sort the body. Billy helped her because I refused to. I was a mess. I left that night and didn't go back. I was on the streets for a couple of nights. Then a police officer found me and took me to a shelter."

"Do you know why she killed the girl?"

"Jealousy. The girl was perfect, and she didn't like it. I lost touch with both of them for a while after that." Marsh swallowed hard. "I joined the police, carried on with my life and improved it at every chance I got. But Billy stayed with her. He always has. I thought the pair of them would be dead by now. But I found out two years ago that they weren't. They found me on a night out in Derby, and—" Marsh couldn't hold in the tears anymore, and she let them flow down her cheeks.

Hart shoved another tissue into her hand.

"My life is over now, though. I know. It's OK. I deserve to go to prison for keeping it all a secret. If I'd have said something, she wouldn't have carried on killing. Many people are dead because of me. Even that night out in Derby, she killed Cara Percy in a rage after I walked off to get away from them. Billy stays with her even though he found his actual family in the end. His brother was in a psychiatric hospital or something."

She felt Hart's hand squeeze hers again. "You were a scared child, and you've helped loads of people since. It's literally your entire life to help people. I know that. I've worked with you. I've watched you. I've seen your heart."

Marsh couldn't resist a sudden urge to lean forward. Her lips met Hart's before she could stop herself. She enjoyed a second of immense pleasure at the softness of Hart's lips against her own. But Hart yanked away. Heat inflamed Marsh's cheeks as she realised what had happened. She clapped a hand over her mouth.

"I'm sorry. Oh my god, Hart. I'm so sorry. I don't know what came over me."

"It's OK, really. Don't worry about it. But I can't kiss you because I'm seeing someone else now. It wouldn't be fair to them."

Her words wrapped around Marsh's heart and tugged hard. She'd known Hart was seeing someone – that had been obvious. But she didn't think for one second it was anything serious. She said nothing, her head lowered. How was she going to get out of this awful situation? She couldn't.

She was doomed to be a police officer stuck on the wrong side of the bars. Probably for life.

Hart stood up, releasing an enormous sigh. This was it. All the blood rushed to her feet, like she was a dead weight. Marsh was too scared to move. This was where Hart suggested going to the interview room and making the interview official, and everyone would learn the truth. They would all know everything. The death of her parents, the foster mum, Lee and Marcie. If only she could drop dead right here on the spot.

"So, who attacked Marcie the other night? Was it you, or Billy?"

Marsh took a deep breath, and held it. Maybe if she held it long enough, she would pass out and never wake up. She could die right here on the floor. With a woman she loved and in a building she loved. Her lungs ached and begged her to breathe as she imagined how good it would feel to peacefully slip away holding Hart's hand.

"Marsh?"

"I did." She let out the breath in one long whoosh. if only death was as easy as just holding your breath. "There was no other way to deal with it, Hart. I've seen what sentences pretty girls like her get, and even in prison she'd keep killing. Hundreds of women die in prison every year."

"Mostly natural causes, Marsh!"

"Plenty are not. I'll be one of them, one day."

Hart cocked her head. "One of what?"

"The death toll. I don't expect you to understand but I just wanted Marcie to be at peace. My sister is tortured on the inside. She will never be happy until she's at peace, and the only way that will happen is death. Life has been too hard on her. And I know I'll die in prison for what I've done to her and for ignoring what she did. But it was the only way I knew how to help her and to stop her from hurting others."

"No. You won't die in prison. You won't be one of those figures," Hart replied quietly.

"Of course I will. I've covered up God knows how many murders and tried to kill my own sister! The media will have a field day dragging the police through the mud. They love to make us look incompetent. Imagine the headlines-"

"Just go, Marsh." Hart cut her off.

Marsh looked up at her in surprise. Did Hart just tell her to go? Probably just wishful thinking. Even her brain was playing tricks on her now.

"What? Where? Go to the interview room, you mean?"

"You heard me. Just go. No one knows what you've told me. Just leave, quickly before I change my mind. I'm going to make a cup of tea, and I want you gone when I return." And with that, Hart turned and stalked right out of the room, leaving the door wide open.

Marsh faltered. Was she really going to walk out of here? She stood, knees like jelly, and forced her legs to the doorway before she had too much time to think it through. She hadn't even reached the worst part of her story, but that was OK. There was only one thing left to do now. Only one more person to kill, and then it will all be over.

Swanson

The early afternoon traffic forced Swanson to roll his car to a stop. The low sun glared directly at him through the windscreen, making him scowl further. He slapped the sun visor down with an angry thud.

"What the hell is with this traffic?" he muttered, throwing a hand toward the long queue of vehicles trying to get across Burton Road roundabout and onto Lara Croft Way – named after the video game character who was created in a nearby office, though that office had long since shut down.

"The end of the lunchtime rush, I guess?" Summer replied, pulling down her own sun visor in a far calmer manner.

"It's worse than usual, though. It's going to take ages to get back to the station at this rate."

"I always enjoy being on this road," Summer replied in a faraway voice.

"Why?" Swanson scoffed.

"Lara Croft Way. It reminds me of my dad. We used to play the game together when I was a kid. I loved it." She smiled, lost in the memory. Swanson said nothing – deterred by the mention of her father, but simultaneously happy she'd shared some information about him. He tried to think of something poignant to say.

"That's cool. It's a good game." He reached forward and pressed a few buttons on the centre console, and the sound of a dial tone filled the car.

"Hey," Hart answered on the first ring, though her greeting didn't have its usual snappiness about it.

"Hey, do you still have Marsh with you? Marcie ran off from the hospital this morning. She snuck out when they were having a morning meeting, No one there knows where she's gone. A nurse said she was going home, but she didn't have the address. We need to get it from Billy or Marsh."

Hart hesitated. "Marsh is still in your office. We're not finished talking, I'm just in the kitchen making tea." Her voice trembled as she spoke.

"Are you OK?" Summer asked.

"Yes, of course," Hart snapped without hesitation, sounding much more like her usual self. "I'll ask her if she has Marcie's address. Hang on."

They heard footsteps as Hart walked down the corridor to Swanson's office. The traffic inched slowly forward towards the roundabout. As Swanson maneuvered into the correct lane, Hart's cursing filled the car.

"What is it, Hart?" Swanson bellowed out over her shouting.

"She's gone too!" Hart yelled. "I'll go check the car park."

More cursing filled the car, this time from Swanson. Summer's mouth dropped open, and it occurred to Swanson that he rarely swore around her. That would change if they worked together. She glanced at him with wide eyes.

"Don't panic. I'll ask Billy. He'll know the address," she said.

It took another ten minutes before Swanson and Summer arrived at the station. Hart met them outside, where she was pacing around the car park, her face scrunched. Swanson abandoned his car somewhere near the front steps, ignoring the voice in the back of his head calling out to him to move it somewhere safer.

"I'm going to talk to Billy with Summer," Swanson called out to Hart as he and Summer jogged towards her. "Can you go get him and bring him to interview room one, please?"

Hart didn't reply but ran inside the building to get Billy. Summer stopped jogging and put a hand on Swanson's chest. "Right. *I'll* do the talking. He isn't going to answer if you ask," she said adamantly.

Swanson looked down at Summer. He half wished he hadn't involved her in this mess, but there was certainly a benefit to her being by his side. She put her hand gently on his arm.

"Don't worry, I'll get it out of him," she said.

Marsh

arsh drove across Lara Croft Way at a rapid pace. All the traffic headed in the opposite direction, and she swerved in and out of lanes to avoid the rest. It's not like getting a speeding fine would matter. She'd be in prison, anyway.

She let the warm tears fall down her cheeks. The soft tickle as they fell was nice. They were human. A last taste of innocence before she saw Marcie again and committed the worst crime a human could ever commit.

All whilst still wearing her police uniform.

Nerves pulled her insides at the thought of how Marcie was going to react. At least Billy wasn't there today. He watched her nervously last time, and she knew he'd choose Marcie over her. He always had. She was his obsession. As much as he loved Marsh, it was tenfold when he looked at Marcie.

She'd watched Marcie for a while before finding out where she and Billy lived. The last time she'd turned up, they'd both trusted her not to hurt them. She didn't hurt Billy, of course. The thought was unthinkable. She hated seeing him being questioned for crimes Marcie had committed, and had tried to get in the interview room before Summer to tell him to keep his mouth shut. But he ignored her, of course. And that note on Swanson's car hadn't worked as well as she'd hoped. But she had made tea and spiked Billy to sleep, along with Marcie. He wouldn't allow any harm to come to Marcie, otherwise.

This time, Marcie would expect it. There wouldn't be any sleeping. She'd have to be quicker.

She flew across the roundabout and up Normanton Road. Marcie and Billy lived just off a side street, which Marsh stopped at the bottom of in order to collect her thoughts. As it stood, Marcie may just fly at her with a knife. In a one-on-one fight, Marcie would win. She was lethal. Marsh was trained to arrest someone, sure, but she was a peacemaker, not a murderer. Not deep down. She'd have to sweet talk Marcie first. Apologise, maybe. Win her trust again somehow.

She pulled off her jacket and grabbed around in the backseat for something to shove on over her top. A dark blue hoodie came to hand, and she whipped it on. There were white Skechers under the driver's seat, too. She flicked off her black shoes and tied up the trainers.

The car door slammed behind her as she got out of the car and forced her legs to walk down the street. If she hesitated now, she'd never make it. Marcie lived at the other end of the street, roughly twenty houses down. She didn't bother to hide her face from passers-by. It crossed her mind that they were potential witnesses. But then again, no one around here would talk to the police. And after what she'd told Hart, she was unlikely to get away with anything. She may as well hand herself in straight after.

It occurred to her that Marcie might be watching out for her through the window. She stepped to the left-hand side of the pavement, pulling her hood tighter over her face and lowering her head. Someone had boarded the top window of the property up, so she couldn't be watching from there. Her hands were sweaty as she reached out to open the small gate at the front of the overgrown yard. She dashed down the path to the front door and raised a balled fist to knock on the door.

She hesitated in mid-air and leaned closer to the dirt-engulfed door. The smell of cigarettes drifted through. She listened intently, blocking out the busy road and nearby footsteps. There was only silence.

She unravelled her fist and slowed her hand to drift down toward the door handle. Still listening, she pushed down on the door handle gently, and it popped open with little noise. The pungent cigarette smell flew straight to her chest, making her breathing tight. Someone had smoked a lot here lately.

It revealed a tiny hallway with aged, green wallpaper and a frayed, beige carpet. Photos of strangers lined the walls; she could see no pictures of Marcie or Billy. It wasn't until she let go of the door handle, she realised how sweaty her hand actually was. She wiped her palms on her jumper and closed the door behind her with a gentle thud. The noise of the traffic disappeared.

In front of her were stairs to the right and a corridor to the left. A door was also on the left, and she knew from her last visit that this was the living room. At the end of the corridor was the kitchen. The house was silent, but someone had clearly had a cigarette recently. Thin trails of smoke still spiralled in the air, coming from the direction of the kitchen. Marsh held her breath as she tried hard not to cough, and stepped silently along the corridor.

She peeked her head around the door at the end of the corridor. The shabby kitchen was bigger than you'd expect from the outside. It was covered in the typical oak cupboards of the '90s and an ancient lino floor. A wooden table sat in the middle of the room, with just enough space for four chairs. And in the furthest chair along, sat Marcie. Her dyed black hair was tied back, and she had a cigarette in hand. She didn't look up as Marsh entered, and instead stared down at the floor.

"I haven't had a cigarette all week," she said in her soft, childlike voice. "And here you come to ruin it."

Marsh said nothing. This was a bad idea. Everything in her body told her to run. She shouldn't be here. She should have been more prepared. She should have sat calmly and thought of a plan for every scenario. Marcie's eyes flicked towards Marsh.

"Aren't you at least going to apologise for what you did to me?" she asked.

Her words ignited something deep within Marsh. A hatred born from betrayal and buried so deep she'd almost forgotten it existed.

"Apologise?" she spat.

"Yes, apologise. You almost killed me!" Marcie looked at her with big, innocent eyes brimmed with tears. "Your own sister. Your *only* sister. After everything I did for you."

Marsh's fist balled, her jaw clenched. "Marcie." She attempted to speak softer, trying to regain control.

"Don't you *'Marcie'* me," she replied, sucking in a sob. "*Sister.* That's what you should call me."

"You're a murderer!" Marsh exploded, unable to keep her composure any longer.

"So are you!" Marcie yelled back.

Swanson

S wanson peered over at Summer as they waited for Hart to bring Billy through. Her knee bounced nervously up and down. He reached over and put a hand on her thigh, and her leg froze. She flashed an apologetic look at him.

"Sorry, I know it's annoying. It's a nervous habit I got from my dad." She smiled and looked away. Swanson concealed his surprise at the second mention of her father. He knew nothing about him before today, other than a car accident took his life when Summer was around ten years old.

"It's not annoying. And it's OK. Marsh will be fine. She can handle herself," he replied, gripping her thigh before removing his hand and hoping to god he was right. Marsh was always fiercely independent. Fair. *Good.* He didn't know the full story yet, but he knew she was good-hearted and could look after herself. That was enough.

Billy's distinct shuffling footsteps trickled down the corridor, and Swanson prepared himself to begin the recording. His miserable, pale face appeared in the doorway seconds later. But the look of sorrow on his plain features soon turned to anger as he noticed Swanson was the one sitting next to Summer today. He stopped dead just past the doorway.

"Where is Charlie Marsh?" Billy directed his question

towards Summer rather than Swanson. And she answered before Swanson could even think of a response.

"She nipped out," she replied in a no-nonsense tone. Swanson had heard that tone before; her mum voice. Not to be messed with.

Billy shuffled forward again towards the empty chair which sat across from the table.

"Is she OK?" he asked, still refusing to look at Swanson.

"Why wouldn't she be?" Summer asked, a feigned expression of confusion plastered on her face.

She was getting better at lying already. But Billy shrugged as usual and didn't respond. He pointed his stubborn face at the table and refused to look at either of them. Summer glanced at Swanson, trying to convey an unspoken question.

He had no clue what she was trying to say, but he gave a slight nod of his head. Whatever she wanted to try, it was likely to be a better option than jumping across the table to throttle the answers out of Billy – and losing his job in the process. Summer returned her gaze to the forlorn-looking Billy and cleared her throat.

"Billy, we need your help. I need your help. I think Marcie is in danger." Her voice was softer this time, and it worked. Billy's head shot up at the mention of Marcie's name.

"Why would she be in danger?" he asked, his eyes wide.

"She left the hospital without being discharged by a doctor. She has a serious injury and could be in a poor state. We believe she went home, but we don't know where that is. We need to know where she is staying at the moment in order to help her. And that's why I've asked to see you. You can help us, Billy. Help us help Marcie."

Billy's face now resembled the whitest of cotton sheets,

having been getting ever paler with each word Summer spoke. A suspicious sweaty sheen had arisen across his forehead, and Swanson leaned backwards to ensure he wasn't in the firing line of any stomach contents.

"Billy, will you help us help Marcie?" Summer repeated softly, and he raised his head to meet her gaze.

"Marcie and Charlie are *both* gone?" he asked.

"Yes," Summer answered calmly, trying to ensure Billy matched her soft energy.

But Swanson saw the crazed look in his eyes and jumped up just as Billy did. His eyes were wild, and his chest heaved as he took in huge gasps of air.

"Hey, Billy. Calm down. Now!" Swanson commanded, ready to pin the little scrote down if he got anywhere near Summer.

Billy responded by pointing a long, dirty finger at Swanson and shouting so hysterically that Hart flung open the interview room door to check on them.

"You need to find her! She's dangerous. She'll kill her. Please find her," he yelled, spittle spraying from his mouth and landing on the table.

Hart stood in the doorway with her body tensed, ready to spring into action if necessary. Summer had stood too by this point, and she moved a step behind Swanson. Though she continued to try her best to calm Billy down.

"It's OK, Billy. We were just talking to Charlie Marsh, and she was fine," she told him firmly.

"Charlie? No, not Charlie. She isn't in danger. I mean Marcie! Charlie is the one who attacked her, OK? Not me. I lied. I was trying to protect them both, but you need to find Marcie to save her from Charlie!"

Summer looked at Swanson. He could feel her confusion.

192

What the hell was going on with these three? Marsh would never attack Marcie like that. She wouldn't hurt anyone. She'd arrest them.

"OK. We'll find them both if you can tell us the address?" Swanson replied.

"It's sixty-two Silver Street, Normanton. Let me come with you? Please! I was lying about the murders. It wasn't me. It was Charlie, it was all Charlie Marsh. She killed them all!"

The splitting pain which ran across Swanson's forehead informed him that was all the shouting he could take right now.

"Billy!" he demanded in as calm a voice he could muster. "Calm down. We're going to find them, OK? And then we will sort this sorry mess out together. Now, I'm going to call an officer to take you back to your room, and I personally will go to the address and talk to them both. You are not going anywhere. Please sit down."

Billy did as he was told without argument, but continued to glare at Swanson. Swanson ended the recording and turned to Summer, nodding his head towards the door to indicate for her to leave first. He felt Billy's eyes on the back of his head as he passed through the door. He closed the door behind him and whispered urgently to Hart, who was practically hopping with impatience and wore a scowl that rivalled Billy's.

"Let's go. I'll explain in the car." He turned to face Summer. "I just saw Trent go into the kitchen. Ask her to take Billy back, please."

"OK." Summer nodded and turned towards the kitchen, but paused and looked back at him. "Then what? I'll meet you in the car park?"

Swanson jerked his head. "The car park? No, I need you to

explain everything to Murray."

"Oh. I thought I'd be coming with you?" She pouted in a way that, in any other circumstance, he might have found endearing. But his heart jumped at the thought of her coming with them to find a killer. Had he not just spent the last year trying to keep her bloody safe?

"Absolutely not. It's too dangerous, and you're untrained. Please tell Murray everything, and she can send additional *officers* to the address."

"I'm not a bloody wallflower!" Summer grumbled, her pout had turning into a scowl. Christ, she was even sexy then.

"No, and you're not an officer, either. You're also causing a delay right now by not being with Murray yet."

"Fine." She walked off shaking her head.

"She's almost as stubborn as you," Hart piped up. "Where are we going?"

"Normanton. But Billy seems to think Marsh is the bad guy."

"She isn't," Hart replied with surprising conviction. Obviously, Marsh wasn't evil, but was she completely innocent? He doubted it if she was involved in this mess.

Trent appeared around the corner a moment later, the only person Swanson had seen recently who didn't have a scowl. Another officer, Swanson couldn't remember his name, followed behind her.

"Alright?" Trent nodded at them both.

Swanson nodded back. "Alright? Thanks for dealing with Billy. He's stressed but should be no trouble."

"No worries. Got Smith here with me, anyway."

Swanson let the two officers pass into the interview room and walked off with Hart towards the car park. As soon as he opened the exit, a wave of suffocatingly warm air rolled over them. Normally, Hart would moan about the heat, but she stormed towards the car with a determined look.

"Right, did you google the postcode?" she asked him once they were in Swanson's abandoned Audi.

"Yep," Swanson lied as he brought up Google quickly. "Seven minutes away."

"You better put your foot down, then," Hart said as she brought her phone to her ear.

Swanson rolled out of the car park, ready to drive over traffic this time if needed. "Who are you calling?"

"Marsh. I want to see if she's actually there or not."

Swanson pulled off towards Normanton, praying the sunshine hadn't increased the usual daily traffic with visitors to the pretty city. He had no siren in the Audi, but didn't doubt that Marcie would listen out for sirens, anyway. As would Marsh, if what Billy had said was true. Hart sighed and threw her phone into her bag.

"No answer," she snapped.

"Well, let's just hope we're not too late," Swanson replied, the sick feeling in his gut growing ever stronger.

Marsh

A drop of sweat tickled Marsh's brow. She felt its warmth spill onto her cheek. Marcie wore an infuriating smile as she stared at her from the corner of the kitchen. Marsh couldn't deny the fear she felt, but she stood more of a chance than most of Marcie's victims. Her charm and innocence were how she tricked them, but Marsh could see straight through that.

"Two little murderers jumping on the bed," Marcie sang in her sweet voice. Her head moved from side to side. She pulled her lips into a sad expression and pointed at her bruised face. "One fell off and bumped her head."

"I am not a murderer, Marcie. I'm not like you," Marsh said through pinched lips.

"But you are, aren't you? It's thanks to you driving that big, nasty knife through our dear foster daddy's heart that I am what I am. *You* showed me what I'm capable of. You made me what I am."

Marsh pushed away the image of that monster on top of her. The helplessness she'd felt night after night. The feeling that she had to end it somehow, even though she knew killing was wrong and she'd go to hell.

"That was different. He deserved it. Do you remember what

they did to us that first night? After he took us back to her? I heard your screams when I was locked in the downstairs toilet. I was naked and battered, and I heard you screaming and could do nothing to stop it. You couldn't hear me. But I made a promise that night to both of you. I would get us out of there, even if it meant murder. I was protecting us. I protected you."

"Yes, you always protected us. And once he was dead, I protected us, too. I killed foster mummy, didn't I? You can't take all the credit for killing both of them." Marcie pulled the same expression as a petulant child.

Marsh's hands shook. She balled them both into fists, her fingernails digging deep into her palm. "Yes, but I stopped after we got away from them! You carried on. Murdering innocent people year after year. What you've done isn't right. You murdered that poor rich girl and buried her in Bell Woods because of jealousy! You took Cara Percy's life just because you were mad at me for walking away that night. And who is the young boy in the woods with them?"

"A young boy? Hmm." Marcie tapped a forefinger on her chin, then slapped it down on the table. "Aha! You mean James. He was a runaway, like us. No one was ever going to come looking for him. And he looked like Billy. I needed his ID to protect Billy. Just like you murdered Lee to protect me."

"And you don't see how wrong that is? Killing a child just like us, because you wanted his ID? This is why we're different, Marcie. I killed only through true necessity. I had no other choice."

Marcie pouted. "Oh, Charlie. You've always been a sociopath. I know about your real mummy and daddy. You killed them, too."

Marsh felt her stomach drop. There was no way Marcie knew what happened that day. Nobody knew. "What the hell are you talking about? I loved my parents!"

"No, you've just been lying to yourself for years. I know what you did. I read your file because sweet Ma left it open on the kitchen table the night before you arrived. You were suspected of causing the car crash that killed them. The police didn't know how. They had no evidence other than a cold child who shed no tears and a diary from your mummy."

A knot curled in Marsh's stomach. "A... a diary? That said what?"

Marcie giggled again, loving the power she had.

"Tell me, Marcie! What did it say?" Marsh yelled.

"You mum knew you would kill her one day."

Marsh fell against the door frame, her legs weak. *Mum knew?*

"How does that make you feel?" Marcie asked in the same way a therapist would.

It brought back memories of her own mother sending her to therapy at eight years old. Marsh closed her eyes, trying to stop the twitch that had developed.

"Shutup, Marcie."

"You've been killing since you were a child, and have the gall to accuse me of being a monster! What's so different between you and I?"

"I stopped killing years ago! *I* grew up. I realised it was wrong and I'm ashamed of what I did to them. I didn't think they'd actually die."

"What did you do?"

"Nothing," Marsh snapped. She wasn't going to tell Marcie about the crushed up medication in her dad's tea that morning. Sure, she'd always struggled with feelings. Her weak parents had been little more than pawns. And it was obvious Dad would fall asleep and have a little accident. But die? No. Their death had been a huge shock.

"Did you actually stop killing, Charlie? Because this bruise on my face says otherwise."

"Again, that was well deserved," Marsh spat, the hatred she felt surprising her. It rushed through her veins, ready to reach out and take over. Despite her crimes, and despite knowing Marcie needed to die, she'd always struggled to truly hate her. She and Billy were her only family. That wasn't the case now, though, as she thought about Billy sitting in prison for the rest of his life.

"Purely because I killed a few more people than you? That's hypocritical of you, wouldn't you agree? You hate hypocrites. You're a sociopathic murderer just like me. We should be besties."

"You're dragging Billy down with you. He won't survive in a prison. You know that. Don't you even care about him? He said he's murdered four hundred people!"

"He's the idiot who tried to protect *you* with a false confession. He is a true sibling who would protect either one of us. And you know he's bad with maths. No one ever taught him how to count. It's probably only like forty people." She waved a hand casually as if murdering forty people was no big deal.

"Why did he even go to the police?"

"We had a pact. If anything happens to me he was to go to the police. I've protected him for all these years, and kept him happy." She smirked. "He owes me."

"He doesn't owe you anything. He's vulnerable, and you're taking advantage of him."

"As are you. Did you tell your cop buddies it was you, and

not him, who tried to kill me?"

Marsh glared at her, refusing to justify Marcie's stupid question with an answer. When she'd spotted Billy in the waiting room, she'd assumed he'd come to grass on Marcie. Or to report her missing. Not to confess to all of the murders, including her own attempted murder on Marcie. If she'd known about their pact, she would have stayed away from Marcie. As for Billy, it was likely too late to save him now he'd been charged.

"Well?" Marcie pushed. "Did you tell them? Or did you allow Billy to protect us both, too? Who do you think he'd choose to protect out of you and me, eh? If it came down to it and he had to make a choice. Do you think he'd choose you or me?"

"Stop it, Marcie."

"No. Go on. Who do you think our little brother would choose?" Marcie cocked her head to one side. "You know, deep down it wouldn't be you, would it? Not after you abandoned us."

"I abandoned you, not him. He just wouldn't leave you."

"Yes, because you're a hypocrite. You are just like me, Charlie Marsh. Except I'm not ashamed of who I am. This world has turned against all of us since we were kids. Our dumbass parents didn't care about us, and neither did anyone else. All we had was each other. Until you run off to play at being a good cop."

"And what did you do to get sent to Ma's?" Marsh asked. "I know she only got kids no one wanted. Billy, who set his step dad on fire. Me. You know what they think I did. What did you do?"

Marcie threw her head back and cackled. "I wasn't sent to

Ma!" She grinned as though revealing a big secret. "I was always there."

"Always there?" Marsh repeated.

"As in never anywhere else."

"You - she was your Ma? Your actual Ma?" The sick feeling in Marsh's stomach intensified.

Marcie nodded, her wide grin still plastered firmly in place. "I killed my own mother, too. We really are soul mates."

Marsh allowed the tears to run freely. "My parents loved me, Marcie. Maybe that's what made the difference. They had no choice but to leave me alone because of a stupid mistake I made when mad. And that plus what I did to Lee, that knife going through his heart, his eyes losing their very light, it haunts me every goddamn day. Every night when I sleep, I see his face. And if I'd have known what it would do to you, what you would turn into because of witnessing that, I never would have done it. I would have allowed him to do whatever he wanted if it had saved you from turning into this monster."

Marcie was silent for a moment, and for a second, she looked as though she might cry. But then her hand flew to her heart, and she let out a dramatic, fake sob.

"That hurts, sis. I'm no monster." Marcie slammed her hand down onto the table. "I'm a friend of the unwanted. The only people who die at my hands are those who deserve it. I'm my own God in this world. I write my own destiny."

The last shred of hope that danced in Marsh's heart was ripped out with her words. "No, Marcie. You murder people you *think* deserve it, but they don't. Who are you to judge who lives and who dies? You've murdered because of pure jealousy, and you've brought Billy down with you. You've let your little brother follow you around for years doing all of your dirty work when all he ever deserved was a good life with someone who loved him."

"I do love him! More than you, you deserter!"

"No, you don't! You are worse than our *daddy* because at least he didn't try to murder us. You're even more evil and fucked up than he was. You deserve to die more than he did!"

Marcie was on top of Marsh in an instant. Marsh fell backwards, her head smashing off the threshold of the door. Pain shot through her brain, and before she knew it, Marcie had pinned her down. She might have been weak from hospital, but she had always been far stronger than her slight frame should have allowed. She had a psychopathic strength that took victims by surprise.

"How fucking dare you say that to me. I am a goddamn hero." Marcie grunted each word through the tears that fell from her cheeks. Spittle flew from her lips, and Marsh saw her big sister for what she truly was for the first time in years. A terrified little girl desperate to control everyone around her.

A part of her still wanted to reach that terrified little girl. To hold her hand and tell her everything would be OK if she simply stopped acting out and let other people in. But this terrified little girl had a carving knife in her hand. And white-hot pain engulfed Marsh's middle as the knife entered her abdomen. She screeched in pain but Marcie reacted at lightning speed and gripped a hand over her mouth. The stench of cigarettes on Marcie's bony fingers made it difficult to breathe as her hand crushed her lips.

"Shh, little girly. It's gonna be OK baby girl. I'm your big sister. Remember that nursery rhyme I used to sing to you?" She twisted the knife, eyes wild and unblinking, not wanting to miss a second of Marsh's pain.

Marsh's hips bucked upwards as the pain intensified, but Marcie didn't budge. She tried to move her arms, but they were pinned underneath Marcie's legs, and her strength was ebbing away fast.

"Hush, little baby, don't say a word. Mama's going to buy you a mockingbird," Marcie sang, her soft voice floating further and further away. It echoed off the walls, and Marsh felt her eyes closing as they had done when Marcie sang to her as kids. But Marcie fell silent, and Marsh's eyes flew back open.

Marcie was no longer looking at her; she was facing the door.

"Stay here, little sister," she whispered. Marsh gasped in air as Marcie's bulk climbed off her and stepped away. She rolled onto her side, unable to stand, and felt her brain shut down as she gasped for her final few breaths of air.

Swanson

Hart barely said a word on the way to Normanton. She'd never been so quiet. Swanson peered at her and saw she was chewing steadfastly on her nails. That was new. He left her be and pulled off Normanton Road and onto the tight side street that Marcie supposedly lived on – sixty-two Silver Street. According to Billy at least.

He had better not be messing them around. If he'd given them a false address, he could forget about speaking to Marcie when they caught up with her. The houses on Silver Street started off as small, mid-terraced properties. But the further up the street they went, the bigger the houses got. Eventually they turned into semi-detached properties with long front gardens or large driveways. Looking at the house numbers, Marcie was living in one of these. He slowed down and peered at the house numbers. Fifty-four. Fifty-six.

Hart grabbed his arm and caused him to jolt forwards, having forgotten she was there.

"There's Marsh's car!" she yelled, pointing a finger at a dark Vauxhall Insignia. He studied it as they drove past.

"Well, she isn't in it," he replied.

"That must be her house, Three houses up, look. Quick, pull up here." Hart pointed at a space a few numbers down from

Marcie's place. "She won't see us coming, then."

He did as she asked and pulled up on the side of the road, squishing the BMW in between a white van and a people carrier. Two vehicles he wouldn't park anywhere near, usually. Though he barely noticed as adrenaline began to pump harder. Hart ripped open the door before he'd even turned the engine off in her haste to get to Marsh.

"Hart, wait up," he called as he scrambled out to keep up with her. "Let's stay on this side of the pavement. She's less likely to see us coming then."

As they rushed up the street, the pair kept to the left and watched number sixty-two. The property was a mess. The top window was boarded up, and the garden left to become an overgrown jungle. The surrounding houses were nothing special, but they were mostly tidy. Marcie's stuck out like a sore thumb. An infected one, at that. Which suited her considering what she'd done.

Marcie was nowhere to be seen from the pavement, though. Nor was Marsh. They crept rapidly past the remaining houses. The potential scenarios ran through Swanson's mind as he tried to prepare for each outcome. But at that moment, the noise of wailing sirens rang out across the street like a warning to any potential criminals.

Hart cursed. "She'll hear the bloody sirens. She's going to do a runner!"

Swanson glanced at her. "Who do you mean? Marcie or Marsh?"

She threw him a foul look. "Marcie, obviously. Why would Marsh run? Billy was obviously lying. She isn't a murderer."

He shrugged. Hart was clearly protecting Marsh from something, but whether he wanted to know what from was another story. He thought about Astrid Moor, an old friend he'd helped cover up a crime a long time ago. Maybe he'd let Hart off with this one. A squad car came into view and raced down the street, beating them to the front of Marcie's house. The tires skidded as it pulled up.

"I guess Murray sent them after Summer told her the full story," Swanson said. "Not that we know the full story yet, do we?"

She tutted at him and rushed towards the front of the house to meet the officers. Swanson followed, but as they reached her fence, Marcie appeared in the doorway. Her eyes widened when she saw them, and she turned to slam the door behind her. The two officers in the squad car jumped out and pulled open her gate to race down the driveway.

"Wait!" Hart called over to them, and they turned. "There might be an officer in there. We don't know if she's safe."

They ran across to the officers, and an odd smell registered with Swanson. Before he could consider what it was, Marcie reappeared. Her eyes were wild. She shook her head as if she couldn't believe what was happening. And this time, she held out a single match in one hand, and a matchbox in the other.

"Don't you dare move!" Marcie screamed at them. "It isn't just me in here and I'll burn the whole fucking place down!"

He looked down and saw a dark patch right under his feet. Petrol. The smell was petrol. Marcie was the crazy one, then. Not Marsh, as Billy had imagined. At least he didn't lie about the address. His eyes followed the dark patch along the drive, all the way to the front door. He raised both hands high into the air.

"Woah, Marcie. Put the matches away. Don't you remember me from the hospital? And my colleague, Hart. We're just

206

here to make sure you're OK after leaving the hospital. The nurses said you left without their permission," he called. "Why have you doused the house in petrol? Is it because you don't feel safe? Because that would be understandable after what you've been through." He heard a noise from Hart that sounded almost like a growl.

Marcie's cheeks shined with tears in the evening light. "I know what you want! I know Charlie Marsh told you. You want to take me away. But you don't understand that they all deserved it." Her little girl voice was back as she sobbed harder with each word. A shadow appeared on the hallway floor behind her; something creeping slowly forward.

"Why would we want to take you away, Marcie? No one has told me anything. We just want to talk, I promise." Swanson took one step forward, arms still in the air. He kept his eyes firmly on Marcie, not wanting to draw attention to the figure behind her.

But Hart gasped from behind him. "Charlie!" She immediately stepped forward, and Marcie jumped back and shook the matches once more.

An ice-cold fear gripped Swanson as he realised Marsh was stuck in the house with someone who was quite possibly a mass murderer.

"Don't you dare!" Marcie yelled, shaking the matches in her hand. "Don't test me. I'll do it, I swear I'll kill us all rather than go to prison!"

"Hey, Marcie." Swanson directed her attention back to himself. "We're going to move back, OK? Just put the matches down. Hold onto them, but just lower them. You're safe, see." He inched backwards and put a hand on Hart's arm to urge her to do the same. She was frozen to the spot, terror etched on her face. He tugged harder, and she allowed him to pull her back.

"See, Marcie? We just want to talk to you. Both of you."

"None of it was my fault!" Marcie cried. "I didn't mean to do any of it."

"I know." Hart found her voice. "I know what happened to you, Marcie. It was me Charlie told. She told me what happened to all of you. It was awful," Hart called out. "I know you killed Lee, and I know why. I understand, OK? I don't blame you for what you did."

Marcie stopped crying immediately. It would have been comical how quickly her demeanour changed in any other situation.

"You're a liar!" she spat. "I never killed Lee. That was Charlie. She showed me the way. She was the one who showed me how to fix our problems once and for all. This is all her fault."

Swanson risked a glance at Hart as he tried to figure out what the hell was going on. Could Marsh really be a murderer, too? She'd turned white. Her eyes flicked towards Marsh, who was now close behind Marcie. Swanson followed her gaze and felt his own stomach turn as he saw the blood dripping from Marsh's middle, her hand gripped around it. That's why she was dragging herself on the floor. The blood leaked along the floor behind her. It was a miracle she hadn't already passed out from blood loss.

"Get an ambulance here," he ordered the officer on his right. "Now!"

"Let Charlie come and tell us, then," Hart called, the desperation clear in her voice. "Let her come and tell the truth about her part in it all. Otherwise we'll never know the truth, will we?"

"No! She didn't just kill Lee. She tried to kill me, too. And you haven't even arrested her! You said she told you everything, and yet you did nothing."

"We won't be able to arrest her if you don't let us save her first!" Hart yelled. Any scrap of patience she'd grabbed onto was about to disappear and in her frustration, she pointed right at Marsh.

Marcie turned and spotted Marsh on the floor, but to Swanson's relief she immediately whipped back around to face them. She didn't care about Marsh. She was no threat, not even able to stand.

"It's true," Marsh gasped in a barely audible voice. "I killed Lee."

"See! She's the murderer, not me!" Marcie yelled, now showing a wide grin.

"And please remember, I tried to stop her, too. OK? Thank you, Rebecca Hart, for making at least a couple of months of my life happy." Marsh reached up to grab Marcie's long hair and dragged her to the ground.

"No, Charlie! Don't you dare!" Hart jumped forward as the pair of them lay tousling on the floor.

But Marsh grabbed the matches first.

"Hart!" Swanson grabbed Hart's middle and pulled her back just as flames roared in front of them. The sheer heat was incredible, and an awful smell stuck in his nose as he launched Hart into the road. He fell to his knees, hands up to shield his face from the flames. Thick smoke seeped into his chest and took away his breath. Within seconds, the bright flames were gone, and all he could see was darkness as the pain ebbed away.

Summer

Summer sipped on a cup of mocha in the station kitchen. It felt like she'd spent more time staring at the kitchen sink than anywhere else in the station. Joshua was being picked up by Mamma again, which he was happy with, thanks to all the extra treats she'd be sure to give him for the drive home.

Her leg bounced as she sipped and scrolled through social media, trying to take her mind off the danger people might be in. Particularly Swanson. If Marcie or Marsh were responsible for any of these murders, which was hard to believe, then being anywhere near either of them was dangerous.

Murray had almost spat fire when Summer informed her Swanson and Hart had gone looking for Marsh without seeing her first. She didn't believe a word Billy said about Marsh, but did believe Marcie might be involved. She'd had a feeling he was covering for someone, apparently.

Summer choked on her mocha as Murray appeared in the doorway. Swanson had once warned her that Murray always knew what was being said about her, and not to even think the word Murray or she would appear. And here she was, right in front of Summer. She stood quickly.

"Hi."

"Have you heard anything?" Murray barked, still foaming at the mouth. Summer shook her head. "Well, I've sent a squad car to the address given by Billy. Hopefully, we'll—"

She cut off as the mobile in her hand rang. She snapped it up to her ear.

"Yes," she barked. "What? Fire! How serious? OK, thanks."

Murray's face paled. Summer held her breath waiting for bad news. *Please don't let Swanson or Hart have been in that fire.*

"There's been a fire. They rushed Swanson to hospital."

Summer's legs fell from beneath her. Luckily the chair was still there to catch her. The walls closed in around her. She heard Murray moving around, and a glass of water appeared on the table in front of her.

"Drink that," Murray commanded. Summer did as she was told, gulping the glass in one go. It helped to focus on something, and her vision cleared.

"Can you drive?" asked Murray.

"Yes. My car's in the lot." Summer looked at Murray, confused. She knew she had a car. She'd asked in the interview.

"Yes, I know you have a car. Do you feel able to drive right now?"

Summer stood. The dizziness had passed, replaced with a need to get to Swanson. She thought of his warm bear arms around her, and his tickly beard against her forehead whenever she hugged him. His deep laugh rang through her mind, and the awkward way he cleared his throat whenever he was nervous of asking her something. An overwhelming need to be near him took over her nerves.

"Yes. I'll be fine." She turned to Murray with a determined look.

"OK. You may as well follow me there then, so you have your

car with you if you need it."

"You're coming too?" Summer tried to hide her surprise.

"One of my best officers was injured on duty. Of course, I'm coming."

With that, Murray stormed out of the kitchen heading towards the car park. Summer rushed after her, looking forward to the fresh air. She threw her mum a quick text.

Swanson's been hurt in a fire. I'm going to see him at the hospital. Not sure how serious yet. Will call soon, but ring me if you need me.

"Are you sure you're OK to drive?" Murray yelled from across the car park. Summer nodded. "OK. See you there."

The drive to the hospital dragged into the longest ten minutes of Summer's life. She took deep breaths the whole way, holding back tears. Every time the worst possible scenario entered her mind, she pushed it away and imagined herself hugging Swanson instead when she saw he was OK. He'd be sitting up in a hospital bed giving her his stupid grin and drinking Fanta Lemon. Hart would be next to him, glaring because she was upset he got hurt and would somehow blame him. It will take weeks for her to forgive him for scaring her.

She abandoned her car somewhere on the grass near the emergency centre and made it to the entrance a few seconds before Murray. She spotted Hart slouched in a chair in the waiting area, and she froze, rooted to the spot in the middle of the reception.

She'd never seen Hart look anything other than immaculate. Yet she was covered in dark ash, her hair thick with dirt. She stared at the floor, blood trickling down her face from a fresh cut above her eye. Her eyes were bloodshot and filled with tears.

Summer's heart dropped, and she didn't run towards Hart like she'd imagined in the car. She didn't want to go anywhere near her. Once she did, she would know why Hart was so upset, and she wasn't ready to hear that. She wasn't ready to lose Swanson.

But Murray rushed by her and ran straight over to Hart. She bent down, one hand on Hart's cheek and the other on her shoulder. Hart let go of her composure and sobbed into Murray's chest as she consoled her. Time stopped as Summer watched them, still not wanting to move. Not wanting the news.

At some point, Hart took a breath and raised her head. She spotted Summer standing there, frozen in fear, and pulled back from Murray. Summer saw her lips move, but she couldn't hear the words.

Or didn't want to hear the words.

Murray stood and gave Hart one last squeeze of her shoulder. She turned towards Summer. Her lips were moving too. Summer backed away, struggling to get her breath. No. She had to get out of here. Get away from them. That was the only way to stop this from happening.

"Summer!" Murray snapped so loudly that it was impossible to ignore her any longer. "It *isn't* Swanson." She felt an icy hand on each cheek as Murray reached her and turned her face towards her own.

"Did you hear me? Swanson is stable. He's OK."

"But…" Summer couldn't wrap her tongue around the words. She pointed at Hart, still heartbroken.

"It was Charlie Marsh. Charlie set the fire and killed herself and Marcie. Everyone else is OK. But Charlie and Marcie are gone."

213

The Change - 15 Years Before

The cold ground had completely numbed my legs, even through the cardboard I sat on. I curled my knees up to my chin and watched as the tears made dark circles on my jeans. I sniffed and wrapped my frozen fingers up inside the cuffs of my coat. Or Marcie's coat, I should say. I grabbed it on the way out of the flat yesterday. Now it was mine, because I was never going back to them.

My tears weren't just for me, but for Billy and Lauren too. Lauren was no more. A sweet monster who thought life was meaningless had replaced her. Marcie had to have control constantly, and what stronger control is there than the power to take someone's life. A power I'd shown her when I pushed that knife through Lee's chest.

And a power I'd always understood. I felt it as a child as I let bugs crawl over my fingers before squishing them. Slowly. I could see the exact moment they lost their battle to live. Most people's memories of caravan holidays as a kid comprised making new friends and having fun. I had no friends, but I remember holding dragon flies still and ripping off their legs one by one.

I'd wanted to see what it was like to do that to a human. And as soon as little Cherry Wilson joined our year, I knew she was mine. She was so trusting, she'd willingly followed me into the woods after school. She didn't even know the woods, having just moved to town. But we played hide and seek. I saw her feet sticking out from behind a tree. And I realised I needed a better plan. So I ran away and left her there. I never saw her at school again.

But she blabbed about me. I still remember the look in Mum's eyes as she asked me what happened in the woods. I lied, of course. Told her I never even spoke to Cherry. But she didn't believe me. My own mum. I wanted to teach her a lesson.

But these memories only reminded me I am the one who should die as I sat alone, shivering on the freezing ground. I'd never meant for my parents to die. I just thought they'd get a scare and be reminded not to accuse me of lying again. If I'd have known what would happen, I wouldn't do any of it again. I'd be nice to everyone, even the stupid dragonflies. After losing control for so many years to Ma and Lee, I knew now how wrong it was to take that control away. I only wish I could show Marcie why it was wrong.

I fingered the short blade in my pocket. On the way out of the flat I'd grabbed it for protection, but maybe it was the world who needed protecting from me. I pulled it out of my pocket and held it against my wrist. It tickled as I pulled it gently across my vein, wondering what it would feel like to dig in. How much would it hurt?

"That's not a good idea, miss," a man's voice made me jump.

I looked up to see a police officer. He was tall and old, at least fifty, with a short grey beard. I felt an urge to get up and run. But I wouldn't make it past him, and behind me was a dead end. So instead I froze - knife still against my skin.

215

"Don't make a rash decision, just talk to me," he smiled sweetly. He reminded me of those kind grandad's from the TV. But I knew what the police were really like. I still remembered Ben delivering me straight to a child abuser with Nadene. I wonder if he made money from it. Did he think I was evil like Nadene did?

"Whatever it is, don't do that. Not yet. I can help you," he said.

I couldn't help but snort with laughter. What was he going to do? Arrest my family? That would hardly make me feel better.

"No. You can't," I replied, pushing the knife harder against my skin.

He kept his distance, but kneeled down so he was face to face with me. I pushed my back against the wall and gave him a warning look.

"Hey, I'm not going to hurt you. Or arrest you. I'm going to help you." I could see his lined forehead now, and the friendly glint in his eye.

"You don't want to help me," I spat.

"Why else would I become a police officer?" he shrugged his shoulders.

"To abuse people," I replied.

To my surprise, he laughed.

"No." He shook his head. "To help people. Tell me what's happened? What is so bad that it could be worth ending your young life over?"

"And what's the point in living if you're alone? No family. No friends. No job."

"You don't have to be alone. There are plenty of places to make friends. I make friends every day, even as a police officer."

216

I released the pressure from the knife - just a little. "You do?"

"Of course. We're friends now." He replied with conviction. I had to admire his confidence. Maybe if I had that I wouldn't be such a twisted loner.

"Nobody ever wants to be my friend."

"I do. I'm Gary. Gary Sneddon."

He stuck out a hand, and I clutched the knife harder. He grinned, showing a set of white teeth. I eyed him warily.

"It's OK, love," he said. "I don't bite."

I kept hold of the knife, but took it away from my wrist and inched forward to shake his hand.

"See? Now we're friends. Give me the knife, and I'll take you to some place to stay for the night."

"Where?" I asked.

"A shelter down the road. You'll be safe, don't worry."

I held the knife close to my chest as I stood.

"You can't go inside with a weapon."

"What if you're lying to me? You might arrest me as soon as I give it to you."

"I have no reason to lie to you. I could call for backup and have a truckload of officers here in minutes if I wanted to arrest you."

"When we get to the shelter, I'll give you the knife."

"OK. That sounds fair to me."

He backed away, waving out his hand for me to follow him down the alley and on to the empty street. It was so late, even most of the drunken revellers had fallen home some way or another. I kept my distance from Gary as we walked, but he didn't make conversation again. He walked to the end of the road and pointed at a building across the street.

"That's the shelter. I know they have a space and if I come

in with you, they'll let you sleep there. You just need to give me the knife."

"Or what?"

"Or I will arrest you. I'm giving you a chance here, love. Because you look like someone who needs one."

"I do?"

"Yes. I believe in you. It was clearly fate that I was walking past that alley just as you were about to do something stupid."

"I don't believe in fate." I looked over at the shelter again. It looked like it had heating, and something comfier than cardboard to sleep on. "Do they have food?"

"Snacks, usually. They might have toast."

I handed him the knife and stepped into the road. I heard Gary laughing as I practically sped across the road.

"Hey! Wait for me," he called, but I didn't stop until I reached the door of the shelter.

"You can move fast when food is involved," I heard Gary coming up behind me.

"I haven't eaten all day," I replied. My cheeks felt hot, and Gary's smile disappeared.

"Where is your family?" he asked.

"I had to leave them."

"You don't need them, you know. You can be anything you like all by yourself. Think about it. I want a plan for tomorrow."

"Tomorrow?"

"Yes. I'm going to come by to check on you. I want a plan of what you're going to do. Then I'm going to help you achieve it."

"Why?"

"Like I said, it's my job to help people."

Gary was so different from what I expected a police officer

to be. I thought about the amount of times we'd run from the police as kids. Always terrified they'd find us and trace us back to Ma's death or at minimum, place us somewhere worse. I'd always seen them as the enemy, but here was Gary helping me and he didn't even know me.

"What do you need to do to be a police officer?" I asked.

Gary grinned from ear to ear. "Well, that's something I can easily help you with. But it's a question for tomorrow. Come on."

He reached up to ring the doorbell of the shelter and a light flicked on. The next few minutes were a blur but before I knew it I was sitting with a cup of tea and some toast and Gary was gone.

"I'll be back at 11am," he'd promised. "Have a plan ready for me."

And I would. Because Gary had helped me to see how I could right the wrongs in my past. I didn't want to die. I wanted to live. The only way I could ease the guilt would be to help others, just like Gary did. I might help enough people that it would cancel out everything Marcie and I had done. Maybe my parents would be proud of me after all. Maybe I could be just like Gary.

Swanson

Swanson waited for Hart on Iron Gate street, just outside of the imposing black gate at the front of the Derby Cathedral tower. Despite his usual avoidance of religious places, he'd arrived fifteen minutes earlier than planned, not wanting Hart to be alone if she appeared earlier. His chest was still tight from the smoke inhalation, and he coughed hard to rid himself of the tickle deep in his throat.

He turned to focus on the Georgian walls of the cathedral. That was twice in a year he'd cheated death. Charlie Marsh hadn't been so lucky. And he was almost in that cathedral lying next to her. Yet, all he'd lost in the end was his beard.

At 11:00 a.m., as agreed, a yellow taxi pulled up in front of the cathedral. He saw Hart in the rear seat and watched as she fiddled with her purse for a moment before getting out of the car. She dressed in a black pencil skirt and long-sleeved blouse, with her hair looking even more immaculate than usual. And though he thought he knew her inside and out by now, the expression she wore was new to him. One of devastation, thinly veiled by grit. A determination to see the day through, no matter how hard.

He racked his brain for something meaningful to say. Anything that would be sensible and helpful as she approached.

220

She slammed the door shut behind her and walked over to him.

"Anyone would think you were going to a funeral," he said, before immediately wincing. "Sorry, sorry. I shouldn't joke. I'm not good with these things." He pointed at the cathedral.

Hart gave him a weak smile. "No, you suck at them," she said in a soft voice that was alien coming from her mouth. "But I need your humour today, Krypto. Where's Summer?"

"She's just there." He pointed over to where Summer stood a few feet away, her black dress flapping around her knees in the light summer breeze. "She's on the phone with Joshua."

"Where is he?" Hart asked, but she stared at the cathedral, her mind clearly elsewhere.

"He's at his dad's," Swanson replied, still racking his brain for something impactful to say to Hart – and grateful to hear Summer's heels walking towards them. She'd know what to say.

"Hi, Hart." Summer smiled sympathetically. "Are you holding up OK?"

Hart shrugged. "Sure."

"Good. Let's give our hero a fantastic send-off, then," Summer turned towards the black gate and linked her arm with Hart's. That's why he loved being around Summer. She knew just what to say and do. No stupid, disrespectful jokes. Everything was easier when she was nearby.

"Come on." Summer's voice brought him back to earth.

He entered the cathedral closely behind Hart and Summer. The priest greeted them at the archway, shaking the hand of each person. He was younger than expected, only late thirties at the most, and he muttered small condolences to each person. Swanson shook his hand as briefly as possible and moved on.

Inside, the cathedral was only half full, and his eyes wandered to the large posts and ceilings over ten metres high. Everything was white with a stunning gold pattern running through the ceiling, and unlike most churches he'd been inside, only two of the windows were stained glass. It was simple, but stunning.

It surprised him to see he knew most of the people there. Marsh had told Hart she had no family. Other than Billy, who was in a secure mental health unit after attempting to strangle himself with his own rolled up t-shirt. So Swanson had expected a small turn out. But he thought she would've had a couple of friends outside the force at least. Maybe her intenseness about the job was for good reason.

Hart and Summer sat about halfway down the cathedral, on the edge of the bench, and Swanson squeezed in next to them. The pictures of Marsh on display were all of her in her uniform, taken from the station files. Her police helmet lay on top of the closed casket, with nothing much left of her body to display. A Derbyshire police flag stood next to the helmet. They sat in silence for a few moments until the priest walked down the aisle and took his place at the front of the church. He opened a book and lay it down on the altar. He cleared his throat, hands clasped together.

"It is a pleasure to be here today with so many of Charlie's family and friends, for whom I hope it will not just be a funeral but a celebration of her life. We have come here today to remember and to pray for Charlie, and to give thanks for her life and to give thanks to God, our merciful redeemer."

The service was over within half an hour, with no one deciding to stand and say a few words on behalf of Charlie. Swanson felt an urge to stand up and say something for her, but really, he had no idea what to say. He didn't know her; no one truly did.

But as they buried the body, Hart walked forward to place a photo and a flower on top of the coffin in her own stoical dedication to the woman she'd been so close with at one point. After they'd thrown the first handfuls of soil onto the coffin, the small funeral party headed to a nearby pub to share stories of Charlie Marsh – forever known as a hero who ended her life to save her fellow officers.

"I'm getting the first round," Hart said in a determined voice, then she walked off to the bar, leaving Summer and Swanson together at a rickety corner table of the ancient boozer.

"Was Joshua OK?" Swanson asked. Looking at Summer now, he felt nerves flutter inside him because he'd finally realised something in the cathedral, and he needed to know where he stood.

"Absolutely fine. They've been to Markeaton Park playing in the huge paddling pool they have there. He's going to stay there tonight, so I'll be alone…" She cleared her throat and looked up at him.

"Well, you can come to mine after here, if you like? I can make sure, er, you're not sad?"

She grinned and flicked her hair behind her back. A waft of strawberry shampoo drifted over the stale smell of ale and spirits.

"Sure. I'd love that," she said.

Swanson felt tiny beads of sweat gathering on his forehead. He picked up a soggy beer mat and pushed it through his fingers repeatedly as he spoke.

"Maybe Joshua can come round one day, too? Just, you know, to see if he likes it." He shrugged his shoulders.

Summer opened her mouth to speak, but closed it again.

Her eyes drifted around the room. Swanson's eyes stung as he realised he hadn't blinked since asking.

"Don't worry if you think it's too soon," he blurted out, blinking hard.

She looked back at him. "I think he'd love that. He'd definitely love the fields to play in. He might like it so much he'd want to stay."

Swanson shrugged again. "Maybe he could."

"Could what?"

"Stay. With you. With me. In my house, I mean." The words came out in a garbled rush and set off the tickle in his throat. He coughed, putting his hand to his chest to ease the pain.

"Are you OK?" Summer looked at him full of concern.

He nodded. "Yes," he gasped. "Sorry."

"Don't apologise," she scolded. "Did you just say Joshua and I could stay permanently with you?"

She had stopped smiling and leaned back in her chair. His heart dropped a little. He looked away, avoiding her eyes.

"Well, I mean, not today. Just, you know, maybe in the future and—" He stopped and looked back at her. She looked deep in thought. "Because I love you."

He grimaced as he realised what he'd just said out loud. And mere moments after a funeral, no less. Three words he'd never said to a woman before, and he chose today of all days to say them. The noise of the pub disappeared as he stared at her with wide eyes, awaiting a response. It had been approximately three seconds, yet it felt like three years before she spoke.

"I love you, too," she replied. "And yes, maybe one day we'll come to stay permanently."

"Who will stay where permanently?" Hart appeared in front of them, struggling to balance three pints in her clasped hands.

224

Swanson reached out to grab the third glass, which looked dangerously close to slipping from her grasp.

"Nowhere," Summer said quickly, though her smile widened and her cheeks turned pink. She reached under the table to squeeze his hand. He squeezed it back and turned his thoughts towards celebrating Charlie Marsh. He was more grateful than ever for her sacrifice, and that his own life was spared once again.

Also by Ashley Beegan

Have you read the rest of the series? Check out The Advocate series on Amazon!

The Revelation

Detective Inspector Alex Swanson thought the story ended with the confession. He was wrong.

It's only just begun.

After the death of a supposed murderer, DI Swanson receives taunting notes from someone pretending to be the real killer. His colleagues laugh it off as an attention seeker - until someone he loves is brutally murdered in one of his favourite Peak District spots.

The stakes have never been higher for DI Swanson as he fights to find the truth about a twisted network that goes far beyond what he ever could have thought possible. When another loved one disappears, he realises he has to face this killer alone. Even if it means losing his own life to protect the ones he loves.

The Holiday Home

The beautiful, old cottage in the Peak District was the perfect place for Simone to take a much-needed break following a horrific attack. Surrounded by nature and peace, she can finally relax.

Until she realises she isn't alone.

Her partner and therapist, Theo, insists there's nobody else there. She just needs to rest. But Simone finds out that this particular cabin has some dark secrets.

Secrets that people will kill to protect.

Printed in Great Britain
by Amazon

15312830R00140